The Case of Emil Diesel

The Case of Emil Diesel

A Novel

Inspired by a true story or actual events

Patricia Menton

To order additional copies of this book, contact:
Xlibris
1-888-795-4274
www.Xlibris.com
Orders@Xlibris.com
775891

Part I

Max
2003–2010

Chapter 1

Max thrashed about in his bed, Marie's voice reeling in his head. *They will arrest you if you come back to the East.*

He awoke from his nightmare, distraught and drenched in sweat. He threw his wet shirt to the floor and lay there in silence, staring at the ceiling in the dark. It was not a dream. It was real.

Why did Marie have to send me that book?

Two days earlier . . .

The small weathered package was left outside, in front of their blue door. Sophie, fighting the wind in her face, almost tripped over it when she went to get the mail. She picked it up and ran her fingers over the colorful stamps that framed the left corner. It was addressed to Maximilian Diesel, and it had come all the way from Germany.

Excited, she hurried back into the house, shouting, "Max, come quick! A special package has come for you!"

Max heard her from his office. He ambled down the narrow hallways that opened to a maze of art-filled rooms. He admired his precious acquisitions and had to visit each room. His steps quickened then idled before each painting. He was pleased with himself, nodding as one hand smoothed his silver-colored hair over the thinning area at the top of his head. His eyes were fixed on each piece of art that hung on the white rice paper walls.

In the kitchen, Sophie had left the package on the glass table with carved bronze legs. Max spotted it and rushed over to read the return address. It was from Marie, his half sister, who lived in Burg, Germany. He had not thought about her for a long time.

He opened the package, carefully picking apart the tissue paper that secured the object buried beneath it. He was baffled to find it was just a book. It did not appear old or rare. He lifted it out and placed it on the table. The title startled him. He grabbed a chair for support and sat down. It was scripted in blood red against a black background: *Criminal Business with Art and Antiquities* by Dr. Eric Kreuger.

Max read the short summary inside the cover. Dr. Kreuger was a well-known art historian who lived in Erfurt. His book examines several stories of victims of art theft by the East German regime during the 1970s in former East Germany. He noticed Marie had tagged one of the chapters in the book. Slowly, he turned to chapter 6. He read in bold letters: Emil Diesel. It was about his father.

Why now? He dreaded the words. *I can't go back there.*

He walked away, leaving that chapter of the book exposed on the table. Max entered the small study. One wall had been converted to a bookcase. He had amassed a significant amount of resource books, auction catalogs, and old and new books pertaining to ancient and modern art and artifacts, filling every space. He stopped in front of the paintings on the opposite wall.

The first was a painting by Schotel, depicting a sailing vessel closing in upon a threatening rocky shore. Next were three black-and-white pictures of sailing vessels thrashing about in a stormy sea. The last in the collection was a color-wash picture of distressed-looking sailing vessels limping into the harbor. His eyes fixed on the troubling scenes with a blank stare. It was just like his home in Erfurt—utter chaos. He wondered if this was going to be the start of turbulent times for him.

His stomach was twisting. *Why did he have to write about my father?*

His eyes shifted to the next painting. The seventeenth-century red-chalk French drawing by Huet, depicting shepherds herding goats and cattle, commanded his attention. It was one of his favorite pieces.

Even his beloved art could not calm him down this time.

He continued down the hall toward the large sitting room with high ceilings filled with natural light streaming in from the corniced bay window. Hung on the left blue-painted wall were eighteenth-century landscape paintings next to paintings of stately-looking gentlemen. Japanese woodblock prints decorated the wall to the right. On the wall behind the high-back chairs covered in ivory silk hung a beautiful Japanese gold leaf watercolor. It depicted a scene of three young women conversing with each other. All this beauty before him and the only thing Max could see was a troubled past emerging.

"It's 2003. I thought this was all behind me," he said.

His wife Sophie, walked toward him. She had heard his anxious loud voice. Her long chestnut hair swung with each step; her warm olive skin glistened under the lights. He could smell her fragrance lingering in the air.

In that moment, he took her in his arms and held her close. She could feel his shoulders relax as his head nestled into her neck. She didn't ask questions. She was just glad she was there for him.

"Max, I'll meet you in the sunroom, where we can talk. I'll get us something to drink," she said.

He walked toward the Chinese cabinet and opened the doors. He reached for his favorite eighteenth-century crystal decanter and poured enough Johnnie Walker Black Label scotch to cover one perfect large piece of ice that sat in his Baccarat crystal glass, then he stepped up his pace down the hall to settle into his favorite black leather chair.

Max stared at the Japanese woodblock prints depicting violent battle scenes of warriors on the wall across him. The ceremonial Himalayan mask hung in the center looked at him with a demon-like glare, not to frighten but to protect.

Perhaps the mask could protect him from his past.

His eyes scanned the skylighted room off the deck. Large windows warmed the room during the day, and on cool nights, a wood chip stove provided warmth and a romantic ambiance. On the wall in the corner behind him was the abstract painting of lined black figures, obscured through metallic-looking cubic blocks. He had taken it from his father's house right after his death. Again he had regretted not being there for his father.

He stepped outside onto the large redwood deck, breathing in the four acres of quiet darkness. The silence surrounded him in a spiritual experience of awareness. One small bright light flooded over the grass and onto the garden, which he planted with pride. Only his father had enjoyed flowers as much as he did, arranging new bouquets himself throughout his house each week. He was pleased the yellow daisies and the red rose of Sharon bush still bloomed despite the coolness of the September air.

He welcomed the night chill against his body. When he returned inside, he eased into his chair. He was falling in love with country living. Though only fifty miles from Boston, this small rural town gave him peace. No more fast life in the city. He had mellowed, and he liked it this way.

For a while, he wasn't sure if moving into Sophie's old colonial home was a good idea. She had agreed to remove her quite acceptable furniture and place it in the cellar, keeping only her favorite pieces upstairs if he decided to move in. In the end, he couldn't resist her. He gave in, taking all his precious art and antiquities with him.

Sophie sank into the plush silk sofa next to Max's chair. Her hands rested on her lap as she stared at him with her inquisitive look, waiting with extraordinary patience.

"My sister, Marie . . . my half sister sent me a disturbing book," he said abruptly.

She didn't even know Max had a half sister until well into their relationship. She thought Max was an only child. He spoke very little about his childhood and his family. He was born in 1948 with the given name Maximilian in Erfurt, East Germany, and fled to Düsseldorf with his mother in 1960, just before the border was closed to the West. His father, Emil Diesel, had stayed behind in the East. He was a graphic designer by trade and a well-respected art collector. He continued to live in Erfurt until he died in 1975.

Frustrated, Max saw his new life slipping away.

"Hey, it's okay." She noticed how upset he was.

"Sophie, Marie clearly wants me to read the book. She tagged the chapter about my father." Max fidgeted in his chair, his right knee shaking as he took a sip of his drink. "I already know what it's going to say," he said. "East German art collectors had their collections confiscated by the Communists illegally through taxation, then their artwork was sold to the West for hard currency. My father was one of the art collectors mentioned who had art taken."

She never realized his father was a victim of malicious art thefts. Why had Max never mentioned it to her? Now her curiosity was aroused. She wanted to know more.

Agitated, Max could not believe someone was bold enough to write about the art thefts. The Communists had stolen art worth millions from collectors and dealers, using tax evasion as the alleged crime. No one had spoken or done anything about it until now.

"Max, why are you so angry about this book?"

Max lashed out, his hand clutching his chest. "I was a victim too. I was never able to collect my full inheritance because the regime seized my father's art. I took only what I could after my father's death. I live every day, in this house, surrounded by pieces from his collection. Most of it had gone to the West for currency. The rest of his art is in museums in Germany and in other people's hands."

"Can't you go back and claim your inheritance like the people who had art seized by the Nazis during World War II? You have rights," Sophie said.

He sat very still, inhaling and exhaling, and said nothing. His behavior unsettled Sophie.

"There are very few families who have gotten stolen art back. It's a lost cause trying to get artifacts back from museums, especially German museums. I know this from experience." He quickly changed the subject. "Think of the cost in pursuing this claim. Why bother when I have everything I need here? I'm happy with our life."

He hoped the conversation would end. Max pressed his lips together. He wasn't sure what to do. "Let's go upstairs. I'm tired," he said.

She wouldn't let it go. She waited for a real answer, not an excuse.

"Sophie, my reluctance hasn't been about the inheritance. It hasn't been about money. It has been about going back."

"Max, I still don't understand."

"I'll admit, I did think about it a while ago." He finished the last of his drink then rested it between his hands, looking at his glass instead of Sophie. "It was in 1996, when I traveled with my boss to the cities of Frankfurt and Munich for business. I was curious about Erfurt—if it had changed much when I was there in 1975. I recall I was nervous about going back, wondering if someone would remember me or the events that took place years ago."

He settled back into his chair, smiling at her now. "Our rented Mercedes handled well on the autobahn. You know what that is—the super German expressway. There are no speed limits. Our car reached 120 miles an hour. Oh, the panic on poor Jerry's face as he clung on to the dashboard. It was priceless." A wide grin covered his entire face. "For miles, he cursed and complained. He was so relieved when we turned off the exit to Erfurt, but all I could think about was going home." His knees were shaking. He couldn't sit anymore. He got up and began pacing around the room.

"We parked at the Garten Hotel for an overnight stay—the small hotel I had stayed in when my father died in 1975. It had not changed much. We dropped our bags off in our room and went out for a walk to stretch our legs. We headed in the direction of the Gera Museum that was a few minutes from the hotel. This art museum in Erfurt was named after Gera Square, where it is located. We stood before the main entrance, admiring the impressive baroque architecture of the building.

"We entered the main foyer of the museum. I froze. There stood pieces of my father's art collection. It was a glass case filled with a collection of small German Meissen figurines. The attendant on the floor overheard me talking about my father's antiques to Jerry. I will never forget the attendant hurrying away from us to find a staff member.

"Soon a man approached me and introduced himself as the curator. His piercing eyes went right through me. 'Are you here for your father's art?' he said. I was stunned. He didn't know me. I did not know what to say. I was not prepared to say yes or no. I did not answer either way. I remember I stumbled over my words. 'I am here only for a visit.' I grabbed Jerry, and we quickly walked away. All I could think about was Marie's warning—those last words to me on the telephone when I had returned home from Germany in 1976: 'They will arrest you if you come back to the East,' she had said.

"Sophie, for a moment I thought I was back in the East. Frantic, I looked around, waiting for the Stasi to take me away. It was crazy. I felt so foolish. There was no more East Germany. I put aside the encounter in the museum and continued to show Jerry the rest of the city.

"Jerry wanted to see where I grew up. I pointed out the house to him as we drove by. I thought it was still an impressive, stately brownstone four stories high. Though daunting to me, we all lived so well there despite the times. I did not stop to elaborate on the details. I didn't want to talk about or remember my childhood. The next day, we drove back to Frankfurt. Our trip was over, and that was the last time I thought about Erfurt—until today."

"Max, what happened to you in Germany?"

"Sophie, I will explain it all to you later." His hands trembled at the thought of having to go through it all again.

She could see he was torn between the present and the past. Whatever happened in Erfurt frightened him. She wanted to understand his anguish over his decision whether to return to Erfurt or not.

The next day, in the solitude of his office, Max read the chapter about his father, reading it over and over until the German words were imprinted into his mind. The author's report was taken from many public files and Stasi files, opened only to a few people, as well as interviews from people who knew his father. The Stasi took everything from his father—not just his art, but his passion too. When he read about his father's incarceration, he was so angry he wanted to tear the page out of the book. He was not told about his father's detainment in the German prison until after his death.

Now the truth was out. Max knew of nobody from the East who had received their art back from today's Germany. He realized he had to face his past head-on and finish what his father had set out to do.

Fight for his art again.

Max searched through the handful of sealed boxes he kept in Sophie's cellar. He found papers, documents, and small notebooks—bits and pieces of his father's life. The boxes had been left in his father's house in Erfurt. He had taken them with him when he returned home in 1975. No one had noticed or seemed to care as long as they were not filled with art.

Max was able to pair each document with the narrative sequence of the book. He discovered enough written proof to make the case that the Communists had indeed seized his father's art illegally. There was no doubt. He had to convince the museums too. He was not ready for a fight, but he could not bury the past anymore.

He shuddered, thinking of what lay ahead for him.

Max talked to Marie the next day, upset by what he had learned.

"I know you meant well, but you should not have sent me the book about my father's case. There is no choice now. I have to go back and make it right. I need to get all his art back. Find what you can about my father's dealings with the East Germans in the 1970s. You were there, and I wasn't. I do not know what really happened. I should never have left Erfurt."

Marie agreed and urged Max to meet with Dr. Eric Kreuger, the author of the book.

"Maybe he can help you," she said.

Chapter 2

February 26, 2004, arrived without fanfare. Distracted, Max was almost at their Lufthansa gate when he turned to find Sophie scurrying behind him, her duffel hanging from one shoulder as her hand guided her small suitcase on wheels.

Lufthansa was the only German airline that flew nonstop from Boston to Frankfurt. The flight attendants escorted them to their business class seats. They still wore their blue tailored uniforms, except Sophie noticed there were no signature hats to finish off their polished look.

Sophie lifted up the armrest that separated their seats so she could sit even closer to Max.

"Everything will be all right, Max." She squeezed his hand hard while the plane took off.

"I know, Sophie." He was reluctant to answer her.

She sensed the hesitation in his voice. This was a side of him she hadn't seen before. He was always so sure of himself and comfortable around people. He loved to talk and enjoyed being the center of attention. He was fun. He was confident. He was a take-charge man who spoke with authority, and people listened to him.

She loosened her seat belt and reclined her seat back as far as she could. Thinking back, she knew it was that strong attitude that attracted her to him when they first met at the Harvard Club in 1998. Tony, a dear friend, invited her to join some of his friends for dinner. Tony introduced her to everyone around the table. Max stood up, shook her hand, and insisted she sit next to him. She noticed his voice was a bit louder than most and he had a slight German accent. It did not take long before this handsome, charming man had her telling him all about her life. She told him that her husband had died suddenly three years before and that she worked in her family's restaurant business.

She remembered how pleased she was to meet someone new. She noticed he was taller than her husband, and all that white hair around a smooth baby face gave him a distinguished look—so different from the curly brown hair and outdoor ruddy complexion of her husband.

He seemed a little shy, but when he started talking about himself and his passion for art, his whole demeanor changed. He took charge of the conversation, and all eyes were upon him, praising he was a proud German. His gay male friends seemed to adore this charismatic man named Maximilian.

Max had been in the United States for over thirty years. His love of European art and antiquities brought Max and his friends together. One was an antique dealer, and the professor was also a collector. Max spoke about his art so passionately that Sophie assumed he must be this passionate about life too.

She enjoyed them, laughing all evening as they shared their escapades acquiring great pieces of art and antiquities. She also appreciated art. She visited the local museums and had taken art appreciation classes in college. That was the extent of her art experience.

She wondered if she fit in.

Sophie nudged closer to Max. "Do you remember the second time we met? We went to the inn for a drink and intimate conversation after having dinner with the guys at the Harvard Club. You took me in your arms and kissed me. I was astonished you were not a gay man like your friends. You seemed to fit in their circle so well. And then the rest is history. I'm happy you aren't gay." She gave him a quick kiss.

"Everyone does find our story amusing." A huge smile covered his face.

Sophie welcomed that grin of satisfaction. Finally, she got him to smile. It didn't last long. He placed his headphones over his ears to listen to Buddha Bar on his iPod, letting her know he was in no mood to talk to her anymore.

She opened her German guidebook. She tried to read, but she could feel her tears rising to the surface. At times he could be so insensitive to her, and he was not even aware of it. She realized it wasn't about her. It was about Germany.

In Germany, he would face his greatest challenge—his past. She thought she knew him well. She had learned Max needed to be in control of a situation. He did not like to show his vulnerability or his fears. Control was his comfort zone.

When we arrive in Germany, would he fear that this time, he would have no control? She didn't know. He could not anticipate every move the museums would take.

She continued to read that Frankfurt was the banking capital of Europe. It was a metropolitan city with smart, sophisticated people surrounded by love for the culture, observed in the architecture and museums. Yet its many parks and pedestrian-free areas created a small-village feel.

"Not this time," she said, crossing Frankfurt off the list.

Max rented a German car, a Mercedes, and maneuvered his way easily around the beautiful old city and onto the autobahn. They drove from Frankfurt to Erfurt, about 220 kilometers. Max was quiet the entire trip, not sure what he would be confronting in Erfurt.

Sophie glanced at the speedometer rising to two hundred kilometers, and she cried out, "Max, I don't understand the Germans' love for speed!"

Even at that speed, cars zoomed by them. She held her breath. Her white-knuckled hands clung to the sides of her seat. He drove so fast they were in Erfurt in half the time, according to Max.

The night before, Sophie had flipped through the pages of her German book to learn more about the city of Erfurt, which was prosperous during the Middle Ages. Erfurt had been the capital city of the state of Thuringia since 1991 and home to about two hundred thousand people. It was the main city nearest to the center of Germany.

When they approached the city, Sophie could feel herself perspiring through her jade-green silk shirt. She would soon meet Max's half sister, Marie. She wasn't sure how to greet her. Should she shake her hand or give her a hug? Preoccupied with his driving, Max didn't prompt her at all.

Erfurt was full of antiquated buildings and cobblestone streets mixed in among modern buildings humming with business. They checked in to the inconspicuous small boutique hotel Garten, which Max knew well. It was on a narrow side street not far from the Gera Museum, which they would visit in a few days.

The room was neat, with light pine furniture, simple and tasteful. After the long drive, they collapsed on the goose down–covered bed. Max fell asleep when his head touched the pillow. Before Sophie could close her eyes, she moved closer to Max, which made her feel safe in the strange medieval city.

The loud ring from the front desk jarred their ears. The phone was on Sophie's bedside table. Knowing Sophie spoke no German, Max rolled over her, his hands feeling the softness of her thighs, and grabbed the phone.

It was Marie. She was waiting downstairs for them in the lounge. She had arrived earlier by train from Burg and had checked in to the hotel. Max had called the hotel earlier to make sure her room would be ready for her. Sophie flung herself out of bed and dressed in a hurry with the same clothes she arrived in. Max was already out the door, rushing down the stairs.

Sophie stopped at the top of the stairs to capture the moment. She saw Marie and Max fly into each other's arms, tears falling down their cheeks.

Excited, Max talked first. "Marie, I haven't seen you since 1992 when Aunt Karla died. I remember it was after the reunification." Max realized he was speaking in English, so he switched to German.

"Max, it is your fault we have not kept in touch. You stopped calling."

He hugged her again, his eyes turning away from hers to change the subject. "How have you been?"

They were talking so fast they kept interrupting each other. Sophie could tell they were related. It was fun watching them even though she couldn't understand one word.

Max introduced Marie to Sophie. Marie gave her a warm embrace and smile despite their not understanding each other. Her deep-blue eyes sparkled in the evening light. She was petite and dressed in comfortable black pants and a colorful print top. Her teased blond hair sat on top of her head and was neatly pinned back. Her voice was loud, and her demeanor was full of drama, just like Max. Anyone could see they had great feelings toward each other. Sophie couldn't wait for them to share those feelings with her.

During a light dinner, Marie discussed the appointments she had made for their upcoming visits to Dresden and Berlin with Max. Sophie just sat still and smiled while they carried on their conversation in German. Max did his best to translate.

Marie's investigation uncovered secret police files gathered by the Stasi, the secret police of East Germany. There were files in Erfurt, Dresden, and Berlin. In Erfurt, the department that handled these files was open to people gathering information about their families. She referred to her notes. A request for information was made first, followed by their authorization, which was given to the family members. Then appointments were made to see the files. Sophie suspected they would be returning to Germany sooner than they had anticipated.

"I want to help you get your inheritance," said Marie. She had set up appointments for them with the director of the Gera Museum and with the director of the Dresden Museum in Dresden. She was serious. "I'll do whatever you want, Max."

"You are too good, Marie. We cannot thank you enough."

"My mother was terrible to me, her own daughter. She didn't care about me. Your father did. Your father treated me more like his daughter. I can never forget him."

Max translated in English what Marie had said about their mother.

"How awful for you," Sophie said. She found this difficult to imagine. Her mother had been wonderful and loving to her throughout her life.

Max held Marie's hand. He understood her sadness and anger, remembering how his mother had ignored her.

Embarrassed, she adjusted herself in her chair and threw her arms into the air, screaming, "Forget this drama!"

She and Max reminisced about the old days. It was as if they had just seen each other yesterday. Sophie sat quietly in her chair, twirling her hair and yawning. She felt like an outsider. She had only herself to blame. Max had encouraged her to learn German. She tried to learn and gave up. It was not like her to quit. She decided to try again.

For a brief moment, she wished she had stayed home with her precious Akitas, Emi and Daiki. Her dogs were her constant companions. It appeared Max could have handled this without her.

She changed her mind again. *No, he needs me.*

After dinner, they drifted to the small circular bar next to the lobby. Max had one more scotch whiskey before retiring to bed. Sophie and Marie doubled up on bottled water for their room.

"Time is so fleeting, Marie," Max said.

They understood this journey would take them back into the past, bonding them together—forever.

Chapter 3

With one blurry eye open, Sophie peeked at the time on the alarm clock. She didn't remember pressing the snooze button twice.

She shook Max hard. "Wake up, Max. We are late."

They jumped out of bed, showered, and threw their clothes on in record time. Their growling stomachs begged for food. Marie was already downstairs in the dining room, waiting for them. She was looking out the window at the barren winter garden, looking forward to the colors of spring again.

Sophie and Max followed the smell of strong coffee into the room.

"Marie, good morning. Sorry to keep you waiting."

"Good morning, my dear Max and Sophie. I still can't believe we are here together."

They slid into the sturdy café chairs and drank their first cups quick.

"Let's get something to eat," Marie said.

He took one more sip of coffee. "Now we can go," said Max, wanting to be the first in line.

Buffet trays overflowed with German salami, smoked salmon, and different kinds of cheese—smelly, stinky cheese. There were crusty rolls and dark bread, thick and coarse like wood, and Danish and sweet rolls. The jams smelled so fragrant you had to resist the urge to eat them right out of the jar, while the sweet butter waited to be spread onto the irresistible bread.

"Forget the American breakfast of bacon and eggs. This is a feast, and I can't stop drinking the coffee. It's the best," Sophie said.

Max could only nod since his mouth was already filled with his favorite food. They had eaten so much they had to push themselves away from the table.

"Today at ten, you are meeting the director of the Gera Museum, Dr. Wolfgang Morgan," Marie said.

"Okay. Sophie and I will meet you later at the hotel."

Eager to walk off their full stomachs, Max took the scenic route. They passed by the Krämerbrücke (Merchant's Bridge), second only to Ponte Vecchio in Florence. The fifteenth-century stone bridge of houses passed over the Gera River that flowed through the town. Max would run with all his might past the small wooden houses squeezed close together that lined each side of the bridge when he was little. Today, the houses were handicraft and souvenir shops.

They walked around the Domplatz (Cathedral Square) before their appointment. Tucked in between the old medieval churches were modern shops with long angular windows trimmed with black iron or wood.

Max gasped at the sharp contrast. "What have they done to Erfurt?"

Sophie pulled the camera from her tote. She had to take a picture of the grand Erfurter Dom (St. Mary's Cathedral) that stood on Domberg Hill near the square. It was the most famous medieval church in Gothic and Romanesque style. Sophie had read that Martin Luther was ordained there in 1507. He was a passionate leader who began the Protestant Reformation which led him to write his own philosophy of Protestantism in Wittenberg in 1517. This provided stability and religious freedom in Erfurt, establishing many churches and monasteries throughout the city, giving it another name —Thuringian Rome. The travel guide stated that there were also five synagogues, the first dating back to the eleventh century. In the 1800s, some Jews had come back to Erfurt after being granted religious freedom and built their synagogues. The fifth synagogue, called New Synagogue, is the current temple of the Jewish community.

They approached the main entrance of the Gera Museum. Once inside, Max spoke in the lowest voice he could manage. "When I was a little boy, every Sunday, my father dragged me to the museum whether I liked it or not. I had no choice. Now I realize that those days were some of the few times I enjoyed being with my father. My love for art grew in my mind and soul because of him, even though I didn't know it at the time."

The Gera Museum was in the midst of being renovated, giving way to a more modern twenty-first-century feel. Sophie followed Max through the glass doors that opened into the foyer. There, encased in glass, stood a large eighteenth-century Chinese vase, three feet tall with a matching top cover.

"Sophie, there it is! That's my father's vase. I remember it well. It stood in our living room on a baroque table."

The porcelain vase was painted in pastel colors of green, red, yellow, and blue. Delicate brushwork detailed entire storybook scenes on all sides of the vase, each depicting a mountain, a man and woman, a tiger, and a tree of small red flowers.

"Max, how beautiful." She placed her hand over her mouth, muffling the loud sound she had made. Sophie glimpsed at Max, who was standing across her. He was in shock.

"The audacity to put my father's artifacts on display without my permission." Color drained from his face. He couldn't accept it. He wanted to see more of his father's possessions and all the art that the museum had taken from his father. He realized now that it must have been so painful for his father to sell his life's work to the state to pay taxes he did not owe.

Sullen, Max walked over to her and took her hand in his. "Sophie, after my father's death, I offered to pay the state finance department his remaining debt. They refused. They said I was too late. The museums had taken the art."

She kissed him on his cheek, hoping it would calm him down. "One step at a time," she said.

He walked away, still upset as he eyed the director approaching them.

Dr. Morgan extended his hand. "Mr. Diesel, it is a pleasure to meet you."

"The pleasure is all mine." Max's voice echoed when he shook his hand.

Dr. Morgan kept a safe distance between them. He spoke some English that delighted Sophie. He had been appointed by the city to become the director of the Gera Museum after the reunification. He was from West Germany—a good sign. Max had learned that after the reunification, people from the West were considered superior by the East Germans. He was hoping for a sympathetic ally.

"We still have former East Germans on our staff, Mr. Diesel. It is a political move we have no control of—for now. I still am wary of them, so I watch my back."

Dr. Morgan explained to them that he was aware of the case they were building against the museum about Emil Diesel's art collection and was well versed regarding the exploitation of German dealers and collectors in the seventies by the Communist regime.

"Illegal taxation of art will be difficult to prove," he said.

Max was skeptical. As far as the museum was concerned, the Diesel collection acquired under East German law at the time was legal. He suspected Dr. Morgan believed otherwise but had to remain neutral.

Taking them aside, the director looked around to make sure no one was listening to their conversation.

He lowered his voice. "I have the inventory, the complete list of items from the Diesel collection that was given to the Gera Museum. I will make a copy and give it to you when you return to Erfurt. One request—do not say I gave it to you."

Max was convinced, after reading Kreuger's book and talking to Dr. Morgan, that his father had been set up to lose it all. The documents he found confirmed it. Now he had to prove it to them.

Dr. Morgan continued his appeal. "Max, most of your father's collection has been downstairs in the museum's basement due to the renovations. I want to help you get your art back, but you must understand that it is not up to me. You will have to appeal your case to the state of Thuringia. The City of Erfurt owns the Gera Museum. It is the state that has control."

Sophie and Max looked at each other, knowing it was not going to be easy. They gripped each other's hands as they left through the large glass doors. Max turned back to look at the Chinese vase one more time. He was frustrated. The outlook Dr. Morgan painted was bleak.

Sophie tried to be optimistic. "Wait until we visit Dresden and Berlin. We can decide what to do then."

Back at the hotel, Marie asked to sit by the window. It was a cold day. She sipped her tea while enjoying the warmth of the sun on her back. Her eyes swept the open garden–style dining room. It was hectic. Waiters rushed back and forth while guests chatted away. She didn't want to miss them walking in. She was eager to hear the details of their meeting.

She spotted them. They weren't smiling.

They were tired from the day's ordeal. Max plopped into his chair, ordering first a beer for himself and a glass of wine for Sophie. Sophie eased into her chair and kicked off her shoes under the table. The stress had dulled their appetites. Max clued Marie in about the meeting. She agreed to keep the director's generous gift, the inventory list, to herself.

Max was discouraged and depleted, but he wasn't giving up. This was only the beginning. Deep inside his soul, he wanted to run away and not look back.

"Let's go by your old house to cheer you up," Marie said.

They walked from the hotel to the house, crossing several streets with worn trolley tracks on them. Fifteen minutes later, they stood in front of the imposing four-story brownstone. Three long rectangular windows hung on each floor, framed with carved stone relief arches. The roof was red tile. The front door was painted a deep-red mahogany.

What a shame, Max thought. *It was grand once.* Now it was a small well-maintained office building.

Five steps led up to the door.

"Let me take a picture," Sophie said.

Max and Marie climbed the steps and sat down on the fourth step. They smiled at the camera, their heads leaning toward each other.

They had come home.

Chapter 4

Home is where the heart is. The heartache is also there.

Max had remembered it all. It was the autumn of 1951. He was a curious little boy discovering what it was like to live in a great big house with many rooms filled with all sorts of things. The house belonged to his mother's parents, his grandparents, who lived on the third floor. Max lived on the second floor with his father, Emil; his mother, Zelda; and half sister, Marie. Jurgen, his mother's brother, along with his wife, Anna, and daughter, Marlene, lived on the first floor. His grandfather's wholesale restaurant supply business occupied another section of the first floor too. It seemed like one big happy family.

Each room in his home was filled to the ceiling with art and antiques. There were white marble sculptures of the Madonna, hand-painted Oriental vases, and ornate seventeenth- and eighteenth-century furniture from Asia and Europe. Worn leather-bound books filled the bookcases, along with small Chinese artifacts, jeweled silver boxes, porcelain-colored plates, and little jade jars from China and Japan. No space was left unfilled.

Old stone vases, small carved china, and glass figurines lined the tops of the chests. A painted wooden horse from China and wood and marble sculptures from Roman and medieval times found a place on the floors with Oriental carpets.

Max remembered visiting his father each morning in his library. He had to stand on his toes to reach the brass handle on the door before entering, his tiny fingers turning the handle ever so gently so as not to make a sound. His father sat at his huge wooden desk with carved spiral legs, surrounded by art. Mimicking his father, Max surveyed each piece with his big brown eyes, skimming each one to find a secret prize.

A large wooden cabinet from France stood against the wall next to his father's desk. On the opposite wall, two wooden cherubs framed a small mirror. On his desk sat a carved porcelain vase filled with flowers, alongside a miniature Oriental silk screen. Surrounding the vase was a small turquoise Buddha seated in between a wooden bird and a tiny marble boy.

Sheers lined the windows to let the light stream in. Max liked to watch the light dance across the room, bouncing off each object it passed over. He was only four years old, yet he knew he was not allowed to touch anything. Across the desk was a single daybed, where his father napped in the afternoon.

Large Oriental carpets lay on the wooden floor made from different-colored threads of blue, green, red, and gold. Max tiptoed on the carpets. He was as quiet as he could be. His father liked to work in eerie silence.

Max glanced up at the huge chandelier with brass arms that hung from the ceiling. Staring right back at him was a scary wooden saint or angel that stood on a pedestal mounted to the wall. He froze and tried hard not to scream.

His father would take his time acknowledging him, unless he did not want to be disturbed. "Out, Max!" he would say, his arm pointing to the door. Max would run out the door, shaking from his papi's tone of voice. He thought rejection was tough when you were a little boy. Still he continued to wander throughout each room, curious to see even more.

"Marie, my father should have loved me as much as he loved his art."

"I know, Maximilian." Marie realized there was no turning back for Maximilian.

Chapter 5

No matter how Max felt about his father, he did look up to him. He called him papi when he was young. Max knew Papi was a very smart man. At night, people came to his house and gathered around his father, listening to stories about his adventures and art discoveries. It was just like being at church when he listened to the priest deliver a sermon.

His father ignored anyone who was yawning or moving around in his seat. It was obvious they were not interested in art. For those who were focused and still, he would take them under his wing and become their mentor.

Max remembered watching his papi from the back kitchen staircase. His loud voice, big laugh, and infectious smile captivated everyone as he took them through one of his crazy adventures to find ancient treasure. Max sat on the steps, listening to his every word. Papi was a wonderful storyteller. Yet deep inside his small soul, he did not understand why art meant so much to him.

Max clenched his fists. He could still feel the hurt inside him. He recalled how indifferent his father was to his own family. At home, he would leave them for days, chasing down another piece of art. Max missed him, and his father did not even realize it.

He never forgot his father's constant impatience. One day, Papi was working on a graphic illustration. Max watched him use a small instrument filled with paint; it was called an airbrush. He saw that when Papi pressed it, a small amount of paint came out.

His father noticed Max watching him and called him over. "Max, come try the airbrush. See if you can stay within the line."

"I don't know if I can do it." Max was nervous, hesitating at first. He pressed too hard. A big chunk of paint spilled out onto the drawing.

Papi was furious. "Max, you can't do anything right. You are useless and a worthless nothing."

Max ran out of the room, head down, trying to hold back the tears. It wasn't until he was in his twenties that Max realized he got his impatience and short temper from his father, a terrible trait he endured and tried to overcome every day, especially with his loved ones.

More stories of his father filled his mind. When his father wanted to listen to the radio, he called Max over to be his antenna. Max would stand there for what seemed like hours, holding the wire to get better reception until his father dismissed him.

The Diesels were one of only a few families who had a television in their house. Max was not allowed to watch it. He would sneak over to his cousin's house to watch American shows like *Fury* or *Bonanza*.

"Pay me or you can't watch the shows," said his cousin.

Max gave him the equivalent of twenty-five cents to watch each show, thinking it was worth every penny.

Since he never got any money from Papi, Max would stay out all day, searching the neighborhood for empty bottles. He would knock on neighbors' doors and visit corner shops with his little wagon in hand. He filled it up with bottles and returned them to the grocery store for money. He always had spending money in his pocket and liked the freedom to decide how he would spend it. He became an entrepreneur before he was ten years old.

His father was always helping others who were having a hard time. Max would go with him to visit Diesse, a young artist who was a very good abstract painter.

"Diesse is poor because he spends all his money on vodka," Papi would tell him.

Max didn't quite understand. All he knew was that his father bought many of Diesse's paintings so he could have enough money to take care of himself and to pay his rent.

Papi said, "Diesse is a kind man and a talented artist."

For hours, Diesse would sit with his father, discussing his unresolved feelings about his latest painting. Max watched them from the corner of the room. He saw that his father was attentive and showered Diesse with advice. He became a regular at their dinner table too. Max remembered calling him Mr. Diesse, Not Again.

Max was angry and confused. He could not understand why Papi couldn't help his own family in the same way.

Yet Max liked going to Diesse's studio because it was lucrative for him, not because of Diesse. Empty bottles were scattered all over his apartment. Once a week, Max gathered the bottles and returned them to the store for money.

Years later, Max heard Diesse had killed himself; he had cut off all his fingers when he was in a delirious state. His paintings became famous. Max was glad he took one of his paintings with him when he left Germany and wished he had taken more.

Sometimes, he did nothing on purpose. He figured out that at least he got some attention from one of them when he was punished.

He couldn't stop the memories from flooding his mind. On special occasions, his parents would dress him up. He looked like a sweet little blond German boy in knickers and suspenders, much like the young German poster boy. He had to wait until he was asked to come down from his bedroom to greet their guests. Showing great restraint, he bowed and shook each hand. He could never speak first—not ever. If they questioned him, only then was he allowed to speak. Sometimes, he was asked to sing a song that he had learned in school. After the theatrics ended, he was sent to his bedroom that was one floor up from the back staircase of the kitchen, where the nannies stayed. Later, he would tiptoe barefoot down the stairs and through the hallways whenever the party got loud and happy. He would hide behind the statues, peeking and listening to all the guests. Each time Papi caught him, he would shout from across the room, "Out!"

Max thought it must have been Papi's favorite word.

At dinner, Max sat on a tapestry-covered chair from the medieval times. The chair felt warm and rough against his smooth skin. Manners were important in a German household. Talking was not allowed at the table unless he wanted a smack across the face.

His parents would teach him to hold his fork and knife in the proper way. They would place a book under each arm. He had to hold his arms very close to his chest so the books would not fall from under his arms. If they fell, Papi smacked him hard along the side of his head. Defiant, Max learned not to cry early on in his youth.

One of his jobs during breakfast was to watch the bread in the toaster so it would not get overdone. Max could only watch for so long before becoming distracted by anything that was around him. Max had burned the bread. Smoke poured out from the toaster, filling the kitchen. He got another smack for his carelessness. Still they gave him the job again, and he still burned the bread.

Max made sure he ate all his food at mealtimes because he was not allowed to open the icebox in between meals. Yet there was food always for his father's two purebred Chows. These dogs got the best meat, and Emil's mother made their food from scratch every day. Once, Papi sliced salami for the family. His dogs got the largest piece. Max and the others got only thin slivers. Papi placed cuts in the salami after the last piece was served so he would know if anyone had cut more for himself.

His father didn't really care too much about food. He would bellow at the table, "Stupidity eats. Intelligence drinks." Max did not understand what that meant when he was a young boy. He thought he should eat less so he wouldn't be stupid. But if he drank more, he would end up like Diesse. Thinking that was not very smart, he decided he would rather eat and be stupid.

Max could not place all the blame for bad parenting on his father. His mother wasn't the best role model either. Zelda was self-absorbed. Max remembered she was never home when he needed to talk about school, and his problems were always trivial to her. She was off singing at parties or having fun with her friends.

Mami was beautiful; she had hair black as night, skin smooth and pale, bright rosy cheeks, and red lips, just like the girls on television. Lying on the floor beside her, he liked to watch her dress for a party.

Her foot would nudge him out of her room. "Go with the nanny, Max. You bother me."

She always stayed out late. She never tucked him into bed or kissed him good night. The nanny did. He grew up liking the nanny better than his own mami.

Max had many photographs with the nannies, but he didn't have one photograph with his father and mother together. They were always off doing something with each other, and he was never included in their plans and outings.

One day, he got sick with jaundice and a high fever. His father rushed him to the hospital. His mother was at a mineral-springs resort in the mountains. He couldn't go home or go to school from the hospital until he recovered. He was there for two weeks, and his parents never came to visit him. Max drew a picture of himself and Mami and Papi. In it, his parents stood far off in the background; he stood alone. Max didn't let himself think about those days. It had hurt too much. As he grew older, he distanced himself farther away from his family.

Shaking those painful memories from his head, Max stood up from the steps, where they had sat for the longest time, stretching out his stiff body.

"What a crazy life that was, growing up in this house."

"It really wasn't so bad, Max."

"Oh, my sweet Marie." Max opened his arms and embraced her.

Even though her mother never gave her the attention she deserved, she was able to forgive her. It was Emil who gave her the love she needed, which she accepted with gratitude.

However, Max could not forgive them so easily.

Max was a young boy when Marie was sent away to school or sent to stay with relatives. They were not given the chance to get close. After all these years, they had a second chance, and he wanted it very much.

When they returned to the hotel, Marie checked out. The train to Burg was due soon. It would be dark when she returned home. They hugged each other. There were no long goodbyes because they would see one another in Burg in a few days.

Chapter 6

It had been another long day.

Max and Sophie could not keep their eyes open at dinner. They savored the last drop of wine and retired to their room. They fell asleep in each other's arms, wanting to make love but were too tired to even try.

The next day, they were off to Dresden.

"Wait until you see this city," Max said. "Dresden was the most captivating city in Germany before it was devastated by the war in 1945. It was in the late 1600s that Augustus II, 'the Strong,' gathered all the brilliant architects and artists to create a glorious city rich in music and the arts. Today, it's a magnificent city thriving in culture."

Max continued along the autobahn. He exited the highway onto a winding hilly road that led to the city. All of a sudden, they were in the middle of a snow squall. Max pumped his breaks and gripped the steering wheel as the car swerved and slid to a stop. Up ahead of them, at the incline of a steep hill, was a large eighteen-wheeler slipping and sliding as it climbed the hill. His heart raced. Max crept along in their car up the slippery hill, giving the truck plenty of room. The cars and trucks behind them did the same. When they cleared the top of the hill, the entire scene changed. There was no more ice or snow.

It was sunny and dry. Sophie let out a huge sigh. "What a harrowing experience that was." They went from feeling anxiety to relief in an instant.

At last they had arrived at the hotel. An entourage of flags at the palace entrance welcomed them. A distinguished-looking gentleman in tails opened Sophie's door. Shivering, Sophie wrapped her warm fur-lined coat close to her body and covered her head with her hood, which fell over her eyes. She looked up, brushed her hood back, and saw a grand palace before her—the Hotel Taschenbergpalais Kempinski. She had read that this elegant baroque-style building was built by Augustus II, "the Strong," for his mistress in the eighteenth century and was restored as a hotel in 1995.

Her eyes wandered around the square. Buildings were scarred with black soot, and remnants of walls from the war still lay on the ground. East Germans and West Germans reconciled together to reconstruct the baroque city. Rebuilding began in 1990. The restoration had to be an exact replication of the original buildings. Despite the slow process, in 2004, it was a beautiful site.

She felt the beauty of the culture around her. The Semper Opera House filled the plaza with music each night as the musicians performed Bach and Mozart inside. The original Renaissance-style Semper Opera House had been rebuilt twice since the early 1800s. The last reconstruction was in 1985 in the Dresden baroque style and is considered the oldest, most famous, and still the most beautiful of opera houses. People sauntered through the cobblestone streets, eating their soft warm pretzels. Tourists filled the restaurants, enjoying a large stein of German beer.

Max and Sophie came to visit one of the most famous art galleries in the world, called the Staatliche Kunstsammlungen. The Dresden art collections are in fourteen distinctive buildings, which all belong to this museum institution, including the Green Vault. Max had learned that some of his father's precious pieces seemed to have found their way to the museum.

The next day, they called ahead to meet with the director of the antiquities wing, Dr. Moritz Woelk. He had received the letter from Max, inquiring about the artifacts from the Diesel collection. Sophie glanced at her watch; it was eleven o'clock. The extremely discreet director was exactly on time.

Max was happy. "I love German punctuality," he said.

Woelk didn't waste any words. They shook hands like it was the start of a game.

"Follow me," he said.

They walked through the great halls and down a marble staircase, turning left onto a long and narrow corridor. There she was, on the floor, tucked in against a white marble wall due to a recent flood. It was his father's sculpture—a bust of a beautiful young woman in alabaster marble. Her facial expression and the style of her dress indicated that she could very well have been an aristocrat or royalty.

"I believe she was sculptured in the 1700s, most likely French. Look how delicate the features are," Max said, feeling more at ease with the director.

The director's posture stiffened. "You know your art, Mr. Diesel. Come, let us go to my office."

Through the years, Max's knowledge of art and antiquities had grown. He was so well versed that even patrons and curators at the museums were impressed with his knowledge.

"I know why you are here," Woelk said. "In 1976, certain pieces from the Diesel collection were given to us from the estate by the heirs. If these items were stolen, we are more than willing to give them back. We are a reputable museum and take pride in returning stolen art. You do understand that it is out of our hands. The state controls the museums, not us. We will give you all the help we can."

Woelk looked straight into their eyes. He seemed sincere, handing them pictures of the pieces from the collection—a camel, an ox, an amphora, and the sculpture.

"Let me know what the state does," he said.

They thanked him and left. Sophie was excited, thinking they might have a chance to get their art back.

"Don't be so naive," Max said. "No museum wants to give back stolen art. We have a long way to go. I am the only heir to the estate, and I didn't give them those items."

They took a taxi to the city of Meissen that was nearby. Meissen was the city where world-famous Meissen porcelain was still made. Sophie read that King Augustus II, "the Strong," commissioned the Dresden museums' collections of Meissen porcelain in the 1700s.

While in Meissen, Max and Sophie wanted to visit a medieval castle called Albrechtsburg, which became a museum that housed art that was part of the Staatliche Kunstsammlungen. They climbed the narrow, winding stone stairs to the second floor. In the center of the room sat a huge marble baptismal bath called a *Taufbecken*. This two-ton bath was adorned with carvings of animals like donkeys, deer, birds, and swans—some fighting, some protecting.

Sophie examined it while Max paced back and forth along the length of the bath, shaking his head in disbelief. "My father would be shocked to learn where his art ended up. I am determined to make it right."

They were exhausted. The taxi ride back to the hotel allowed Max to close his eyes.

Their luxurious canopy bed was plush with down pillows that hugged their heads. After a hot shower in the extravagant marble bathroom, Sophie, wearing a French lace negligee, enticed Max to come to bed. She did not want him to forget her. He was able to make her swoon. His mouth covered her body with soft kisses, and she was eager to give him pleasure in return. They fell asleep in each other's arms.

They woke up three hours later, refreshed and ready to enjoy the evening. Sophie put on her alluring green velvet dress with folds of green satin that slightly draped over her breasts. Max wined and dined with her as if it were their first date. She fell in love with Dresden from that day on and often thought of it as her favorite city in Germany.

Chapter 7

The next day, they drove to Burg. It was an easy three-hour-long drive—no bad weather, no heavy traffic. The Gothic and Romanesque style of the city was similar to Erfurt, only smaller. Burg, like Magdeburg, was surrounded by the Harz Mountains; it was called the land of German fairytales due to its cluster of sixteenth-century houses in its valleys.

They arrived at the Hotel Burg. Marie planned to meet them. She waved to them as her car approached the circular driveway of the hotel. Her smile was infectious, and her eyes gleamed with joy. She was thrilled to have them visit her home. The neighborhood was lined with apartment buildings that looked alike. They followed Marie upstairs to her apartment.

"Horst, Horst, come and meet my wonderful Max and Sophie."

A tall and shy Horst peeked around the corner of the living room. He took their coats and shook Max's hand. He gave Sophie a kiss on the cheek.

A sweet, savory aroma came from the kitchen. Marie had prepared a special meal to please Max. It was *Rouladen* and red cabbage with spaetzle. Rouladen is braised beef rolled with layers of bacon and onions then slow-cooked for hours in beer to make a rich brown sauce. It was the same recipe passed down from his grandmother. His eyes teared up, thinking that Marie had prepared it just for him.

A drink before dinner settled them in for the evening. Sophie wandered through the living room. She bent over and picked up each one of several pictures of Marie's family. Photographs of warm, smiling faces were displayed in simple frames on a round mahogany high table. Sophie never understood why Max did not like to display family pictures in their home. He preferred portraits of faces in oil and watercolor, any medium, as long as it was not photographs. Max found black-and-white photographs of his mother and father and photographs of his grandfather that were stored away among old tax bills. There were many photographs of him happy with the nanny. Yet there was not one photograph of Max with his mother and father as a family. He was not included. He grew up disliking photographs of families altogether.

Marie cavorted in front of them, proud to show off her collectibles of handcrafted linens for the table and a fine porcelain plate from her mother, who had taken it from Emil. She presented them with a set of linens for their house.

Sophie studied Horst. He had beautiful brown eyes. Despite his shyness, when he laughed, his eyes laughed also. They seemed comfortable with each other. Sophie was pleased. Marie had made a good life for herself despite her unhappy childhood.

Max saw how happy Marie was. "I did not stay in touch with you. I am sorry. I was never good with keeping in touch with anybody." It never mattered to him.

"I am sorry too, Maximilian."

In that moment, he perked up, his eyes shifting to Sophie. He shook the guilty feeling off as quickly as it appeared.

Max savored every moment—good food, good wine, and good company. After dinner, cognac was served. Max swirled the glass and watched the French brandy coat the inside.

"Perfect," he said. He settled into an armchair to listen to Marie discuss her findings regarding his case.

"The state wants it to become a finance issue because money and taxes were involved. The museums would like nothing more than to see the case move in that direction," Marie said.

"I cannot let that happen," Max said. "We must stay true to our convictions. We want all the artwork back, not the money. We have to prove the Communists took my father's art illegally for monetary gain."

"There are Stasi files on your father. The East Germans recorded everything on paper in triplicate. When East Germany fell, government officials, secret police, and many others were seen destroying thousands of documents. Thousands of copies still remain. Therefore, they keep incriminating themselves," Marie said.

"Marie, we have some of those incriminating documents. We need to show them to the right people. We can prove my father was a collector, not a dealer. We have receipts. The Stasi knew he worked for the East German government as a graphic illustrator. We have to convince the state there was coercion, fraud, and theft. We have the documents. They have to listen to us."

Max was certain that when they returned to Germany, they would be facing a greater challenge—the finance department. He panicked. *It's happening again.*

"Sophie, we have to be prepared." *This is far too familiar. It may not end well this time.* "Maybe the author, Dr. Kreuger, can give us some advice in Berlin."

After many hugs and kisses, they returned to the hotel. They had so much on their minds; it took them a while to fall asleep. The whole evening was overwhelming.

The next morning, they were off to Berlin. Two hours later, as they approached the city, they were startled by the sheer magnitude of the Brandenburg Gate. Sophie referred to her guidebook. She was looking at the original entrance to the city of Berlin. It was built in 1788 as an arch of peace and was modeled after the entrance to the Acropolis in Athens. It became a symbol of reconciliation and hope. It was an awe-inspiring sight.

Max pointed to a magnificent building in the distance. "That is our hotel—Hotel Adlon Kempinski. It has an incredible view of the gate."

"Oh, Max, it's beautiful. Look at the classical style—like a royal country manor."

They walked under a brilliant red canopy. The staff greeted them in black top hats and tails and led the way to the reception desk.

Inside, high ceilings with flowing balconies framed art deco–style rooms, yet it still had a contemporary feel. Elegant silk-covered chairs invited guests to sit and talk throughout the day. It was as if they had stepped into the lives of the rich and famous, royalty and celebrities. It was surreal.

That evening, they met Dr. Kreuger, the author of the book, in the lounge. He was charming. After a polite introduction, they ordered drinks. Max was thrilled they had his favorite Black Label scotch. Dr. Kreuger ordered a single malt whiskey, and Sophie ordered champagne. Since Dr. Kreuger spoke very little English, Max tried his best to translate their conversation to Sophie. Dr. Kreuger discussed the chapter about Max's father, reciting almost verbatim from the book.

He asked Max personal questions about his father. "What was he like? What do you know about his collection?"

Max realized Dr. Kreuger wanted to do more than just give them advice. Instead of answering Dr. Kreuger's questions he asked, "What do you think our chances are in getting our art back?"

"I want to help you get your inheritance, Mr. Diesel, but I need more information about your father and his art."

Skeptical, Max remained elusive. Maybe Dr. Kreuger wanted a piece of the inheritance or to write another book. Max was not ready to share his information. Kreuger recommended a prominent attorney in art recovery in Berlin, Dr. Karl Becker. Max thanked him for his time. For now, they decided to continue with the case on their own.

March began with another disappointment, but they were not disheartened. Max was almost relieved. They agreed not to talk about the case that evening. Sophie looked sexy in her black silk dress and pearls. Dinner was extravagant, with caviar and champagne, but they didn't care. The evening was theirs to enjoy.

For the next two days, they were happy walking the wide sidewalks of Berlin. Street markets flourished alongside the designer shops of Friedrichstraß. They also visited a small museum that recounted the story of the Berlin Wall.

In 1945, at the Yalta Conference in Crimea, the Allies (United States, Britain, and the Soviet Union) agreed on dividing a defeated Germany into occupation zones and on dividing Berlin, the German capital, among the Allied powers as well. The wall was erected in 1961 by the GDR (German Democratic Republic) as an antifascist protection wall made of brick and barbed wire. Checkpoint Charlie was the most important crossing point between East Berlin, the East German sector, and West Berlin, the Allied sector. It was a symbol of the Cold War and fell in 1989.

The story left a haunting impression on them.

Chapter 8

They took the express train back to the Frankfurt Airport, returned the rental car, and found their way to the business class lounge. It would be three long hours more before their flight departed Frankfurt. The quiet lounge was a blessing. Relaxing in comfort made their wait bearable. They were eager to get home. Sophie missed her bed and her precious Akitas. Max missed work.

The plane ride was different this time. Sophie did not have a moment to herself. They played their favorite card game, gin rummy, to pass the time. Max teased her with his dry humor and loud laughter and tried to distract her with sexual innuendos so he could have the advantage of making more melts to win the game. They cuddled and drank champagne. Their trip was not discussed, except for the time spent with Marie. Thrilled to be home, they picked up their happy dogs from their friends and fell back into their routine. Spring would arrive soon enough.

In mid-April 2005, Marie was upset when she telephoned Max. "They won't let me see the Stasi files. Only the heir can see them."

"Marie, I know. I also learned that I will not be able to see all my father's Stasi files—only the files that pertain to his case and the Stasi files they kept on me. It looks like all we can do now is to wait. The museum directors are looking into the case on their end."

Actually, he was relieved, wanting it all to be over.

Sophie frowned, overhearing his conversation.

Max sensed her frustration. "Be patient, Sophie."

Usually, Sophie was the one telling Max to be patient. So they waited, watching the seasons change.

At home, their lives were busy. Max was building his engineering business, and carefree Sophie took care of the house and her dogs. She had given some thought about going back to work, but Max wanted her by his side. She agreed. It was too late. She would do anything for him. This spiraled her into a whole new chapter of her life, closing forever the one she left behind.

In May 2006, they went back to Erfurt, but only for a short time. The trip was all business. Marie set up appointments for them at the finance department, the Gera Museum, and the archive department, where the Stasi files were kept. The finance administrator showed Max documents of tax payments his father had made to the East German finance department before his death from the sale of his art to the state. He explained that it was a tax issue and that he could get money back if it was proven to be an illegal taxation, but not the art; he had to settle it with the museums.

Max wanted his art—his inheritance. He stormed out of the office. "Sophie, I think there is a way to get our art back. I have a good feeling." Little did they realize at the time that the administrator was just appeasing them.

The next day, they were off to the Gera Museum. Dr. Morgan, the director, included six other members of the art and antiquities departments in the meeting. All of them had been briefed about the case. Max presented a book to Dr. Morgan that contained information regarding the Diesel collection and the museum. Dr. Morgan read the marked paragraph of an article in the book to the staff. It stated that in 1975, a collection of German figurines had been acquired by the Gera Museum. It was from the Diesel collection. Dr. Morgan walked toward one of the female members and then read the name in the book of the person who wrote that article.

"It was you who made this statement. You were there when the collection came to the museum. This is your name at the bottom of the page."

Flustered, the staff member pushed herself away from the table, humiliated that she had been singled out by the director. She ran out of the room, never answering him.

Everyone at the table was squirming in their chairs. Sophie assumed this older woman was one of the former East German staff members and still an avid supporter of the old way of life.

The director took Max and Sophie aside so no one would hear. "She has not gotten over the reunification and does not like confrontation from me. We cannot get rid of her right now. She has seniority. I am trying to replace her without creating an incident," the director reassured them again. He would continue to make an effort to help Max get his father's art back.

Max wanted to trust him. "Thank you, Dr. Morgan," Max said, shaking his hand. "I am willing, of course, to leave some pieces in the museum. I know it's what my father would have wanted. After all, he was a loyal member of the museum."

"Maximilian, I was hoping you would leave some of the collection here with us."

"Under one condition, Dr. Morgan. Emil Diesel's name must appear as benefactor of the collection. It was his legacy."

The director slipped Max the copies of the inventory he had promised. They left the lobby of the museum and felt good about the meeting. It appeared the pendulum was swinging in their favor; it was about time.

Starving, they grabbed a bratwurst sandwich at the fast-food lunch stop. They headed to the archive office where the original Stasi files of hundreds of thousands of victims and informers of the East German regime were kept. A gaunt, thin-haired woman approached Max. He handed her his written request as she showed him where to sit. Max waited for the longest time. Out she came, arms full of files. She went back again and brought another armful.

It took him all afternoon to look through the files, and he had not finished reading when it was time to go. He paid for the files he chose for them to copy. They would mail them to his home address in the States. Max wondered how long that would take.

These files corroborated their documents. Emil did pay his taxes on his earnings as a graphic illustrator, and he was forced to pay an additional exorbitant amount of tax to the East German finance department because he was declared a commercial art dealer. He had to sell his art to the state dealer to pay his debt. After his death in 1975, the art that was left in his home was confiscated and given to the museums to pay the remaining debt. Clearly, these facts indicated coercion. Emil was a collector, not a dealer. These documents proved that Max had a right to his inheritance.

One file stated that it was illegal for the government to acquire art from an estate without written authorization of the heir. In other words, they did not have the written permission or a bill of sale from Maximilian Diesel, the heir, to seize the art from the Diesel estate and place it in the Gera Museum.

He thought, *With all this evidence, how can the state refute our case?*

Chapter 9

In 2006, they had left Germany filled with hope. For the next year, it was a waiting game. Everybody was stalling. Max's letters and email went back and forth from the finance department to the museums. They waited for Max to give up. Max and Sophie had no intention of quitting. Max spent hours rehashing his conversations with the director and curator and scrutinizing the documents he had gathered when he was in Erfurt. He wondered if they were just fooling themselves. No museum wants to give art back.

Max's mother passed away in April 2007. Max thanked Marie for taking care of the arrangements since he would not be there. He had tried to make peace with her again before she died, but to no avail. She was stubborn to the end.

Sophie remembered their visit with Zelda in Düsseldorf the year before. They had taken the train from Erfurt to Düsseldorf for an overnight stay, an eight-hour-long ride. Their seats in first class were comfortable and wide and with plenty of legroom. They stumbled through the moving cars to the dining room, where sandwiches and sweets were served. They passed their time reading, talking about Erfurt, playing cards, and dozing off. The train was moving fast and outside the window, everything was all a blur.

They arrived around four o'clock in the afternoon and took a taxi to his mother's apartment. It would have been fun to walk the streets and the wide boulevards, similar to the streets of Paris, but it was a cloudy, muggy, rainy day.

"They call Düsseldorf *Little Paris*," Max said. "We will sightsee next time." It took them forever to climb the narrow stairs. They held on to the railing and dragged their bodies and bags up the two flights.

Zelda greeted them with a smile and open arms at the door. She was a beautiful woman still with great pride. Her black graying hair was pulled back in a bun, and she walked slowly in her flowered housecoat due to her progressive osteoporosis. Despite her illness, she insisted they stay with her overnight, though they had planned to stay at a hotel nearby. She gave them her bed to sleep in. The bed was made up with fine linens trimmed with lace that felt luxurious when they touched them. She made them tea, grimacing with every step, but it did not stop her from playing the perfect host. Sophie enjoyed talking with her since she spoke perfect English and she didn't need Max to translate. Zelda seemed to enjoy Sophie too.

Sophie retired to the bedroom so that Max and his mother could talk. He made a special effort to make peace with her, even though the bad memories were difficult to erase. He tried not to raise his voice at her. It was then he realized it was never going to be easy for him to forgive her for the way she treated him and Marie.

That night in bed, Max whispered to Sophie, "She never really cared for her children. She didn't know how to act around me. Later on, I think she resented me for moving on with my life. She did not love me. She loved only my father. Her interest in his art meant only money to her. When he lost interest in her, she became a bitter woman."

Max wanted to leave in the morning before breakfast to catch their flight to the US. They said their goodbyes. Max hugged his mother for what he thought would be the last time. The weeks became months. Summer came and went. Max corresponded every two weeks with the finance and art departments.

It was always the same. "We are working on it."

Exasperated, he shouted at Sophie, "They are waiting for me to die before they give us our art back!" Maybe the past was catching up to him. Repercussions were coming. He could feel it.

"Call Marie. She will know what to do."

He gave up and called her.

"Now you need an attorney. Call Dr. Becker," Marie said.

"I admit you are right. It is time to call Dr. Becker and set up an appointment."

In October 2007, they were off to Berlin to meet with the attorney Dr. Karl Becker, who specialized in art recovery cases. They entered the modern building that was tucked in among the old, historic ones lining the street. Anxious, they gripped each other's hands as the elevator went up to the second floor, hoping he would take their case.

A pleasant tall young attorney greeted them with a big smile and a firm handshake. Max smiled at Sophie. They liked him. An impression was formed in that moment. He had to be interested in a case like theirs. They had learned that he was an artist himself and had been around art all his life.

Max spoke first. "Dr. Becker, I have exhausted all my resources fighting for my inheritance. I need your help. I was told you are the best."

He tried not to sound like he was begging. He explained the case to Dr. Becker in detail and gave him a folder of all the documents that he had brought with him. He set them on his desk.

"I will look them over and get back to you soon," he said abruptly.

Max was confused. He couldn't read him. Was this a sign of an agreement? The meeting was over. They shook hands and walked out the door.

Sophie pulled Max close to her. "I think the meeting went well."

"I don't know." Max winked at her. "He kept the meeting short and sweet. I like that. He is smart. I don't think he will pass up this challenge, especially since it deals with the former East Germany."

They left Berlin the next day, hopeful that when they returned home, good news would be waiting for them.

Dr. Becker plowed through the files and documents. He contacted the museum directors involved in the case. He knew each of them well. Also, as a lawyer, he had privileged access to look at files Max was not allowed to see.

Max and Sophie returned home. The following week, Dr. Becker called them.

"This is an interesting and complex case, but I think we have a good chance to win."

In 2008, Dr. Becker launched a full publicity campaign in Germany about their case through newspapers like *Der Tag* from Hamburg and *Die Abendnachrichten* from Berlin, including the scandalous paper *Der Informant*. He wanted to generate sympathy for his client. The headline was "Heir fights for art seized by Communist East Germany," with the full story and pictures.

Soon after, Becker's campaign created talk in Germany. A German journalist and film crew visited their home to interview Max. He was nervous as the camera rolled. He spoke slowly in German about his father and his inheritance. Sophie handed him a handkerchief to wipe the sweat from his forehead. His confidence grew the more he talked. Everyone who watched would realize that there was no turning back for him. He knew it too. He wasn't afraid anymore. The talk show aired in Germany two weeks later.

In May 2010, Max and Sophie returned to Erfurt. There were more interviews with reporters and more pictures. The official in charge of cultural policy, Ms. Mitzer, explained at a news conference that the City of Erfurt wanted to reach a settlement. She needed to know which objects Mr. Diesel wanted back from the Gera Museum.

Excited, Sophie and Max moved closer, surrounding Dr. Becker. "Could it really be over?"

He wasn't smiling, only skeptical about her sudden change of heart. She had always treated the case as though the East German regime had acted according to the law.

"I wouldn't count on it. We have to wait and see if she stands by her public statements. Remember, she is a Left Party member and was a Communist Party member during the GDR era."

He was right. Since then, the City of Erfurt had refused requests from him for copies of the listed artworks of Emil Diesel that were held in the museum.

Ms. Mitzer kept changing her mind. He insisted on meeting with her in her office.

He confronted her. "Have you made a decision?"

"Our negotiations are still ongoing. Legal procedures continue," she said.

"We would like to avoid going to court, but we will if you are not willing to cooperate," Dr. Becker said, challenging her explanation.

Flushed with anger, she regained her composure and blatantly answered back, "All the items in the Gera Museum are the property of the Gera Museum."

It was not over despite the drama. Max and Sophie would return to Erfurt.

Chapter 10

In October 2010, the leaves in New England were turning brilliant colors of red and gold. The air smelled of burning oak firewood. In the great room, Sophie and Max curled up on the ivory silk sofa in front of the warm brick fireplace. Bach played in the background. Max admired his Dutch paintings by his favorite painter, Teniers; he had placed them strategically around him.

He remembered the craziness he went through to have all these beautiful objects around him. He could have lost everything, including his life. Even now, it was what his father wanted him to do. He was sure of that. Was it all worth it? Yes, it was.

Max envisioned their house cluttered with artwork—paintings and rare books stacked against the walls, Roman torsos and Greek heads of gods placed on columns throughout the house. He was awestruck by the mystical atmosphere that was created. Max, like his father, had found his passion. It was in his blood. Max couldn't stop his wanting.

"Now I understand why my father became obsessed with his possessions. The need penetrates your head and heart. He let it consume his soul. I am not like him."

"You are like him," Sophie said. "Everything for you is about detail and control. Perfection drives you. Look around you. You aspire to be a collector like your father."

"That may be true. Still I am not my father." He thought of his love for Sophie and for his daughter. "I know what is most important to me, and it is not my possessions. My father could not understand

45

that family mattered more than art. For him, life was always about his possessions. It was his compelling motivation to live. He accumulated it for himself—not for anybody, not for me. Art was his only true happiness."

Part II

Emil
1911–1975

Chapter 11

In the city of Erfurt, Germany, on September 12, 1911, Emil Diesel was born with art in his blood and soul. It was a blessing and a curse. His father was an art collector, but his collection was small compared to the vast collection Emil would acquire in his lifetime—until *it was taken*.

The journey began here.

Emil grew up with a roof over his head and food on the table. It was a secure, somewhat stable environment despite his father's clandestine affairs of the heart, which stirred up problems and caused a divorce. Little Emil withdrew to his room, where he found his peace in sketching and dreaming in color.

His parents saw he had a remarkable talent.

"I want to go to art school," he said.

"We won't change your mind," they said, agreeing that he made a good choice.

When he came of age, they let him attend the local art school. He filled his bedroom with his paintings and drawings and studied with determination, absorbing everything he could about art, increasingly fascinated by each artist's creation he researched.

Soon he was able to understand the passion of artists, like Turner and Delacroix, who shaped the Impressionists of the nineteenth century. He obsessed over their new techniques of color contrast, such as free-form brushstrokes and plein air painting to capture the outside sunlight, which excited the art world.

His parents anguished over how hard he worked. "Emil, slow down. It takes time to become a great artist," they said, seeing his impatience wearing him down physically.

He realized it too. Being an artist would never be enough for him. He wanted more. He made his decision a conquest. He laid out a well-conceived plan and saw his future unfold. First he apprenticed as a graphic illustrator, knowing it would secure him a good job. It was the start of a great adventure. He was only sixteen years old.

Emil's passion was to be a great collector of art—*to leave his mark in the world.*

He dreamed of building an art collection like the famous collectors of the world—the Medici family of Florence during the fifteenth century, emperors in courts throughout Europe during the sixteenth and seventeenth centuries, and Catherine the Great, who established the Hermitage, Russia's largest state gallery in 1763. He wanted the same excitement of discovery and thrill of acquisition. Each painting, sculpture, and drawing became fixed in his memory, keeping alive his passion to pursue his dream.

After his graduation in 1928, Emil developed health issues. It was his liver. The doctor told him it was a good idea to live by the water where the air was clean. Emil was not at all unhappy about his diagnosis or about leaving home.

His parents did not stop him.

He got two job offers—one in Amsterdam, Holland, and the other in Stockholm, Sweden. He wanted to become a part of the small tight art community and loved what he had learned about Amsterdam. He was drawn to the romance of the city and to the story of how, at the end of the twelfth century, it grew from a city of canals in the Amstel River to become an important port and center of finance and diamonds. It was a city of culture and social liberalism. That was it. At the age of eighteen, Emil packed his bags and moved to Amsterdam. His enduring love for the city of Amsterdam lasted thirteen years (from 1929 to 1942).

Emil was hired as a graphic illustrator for a small publishing house. He was impressionable and eager to learn. His boss noticed his natural talent, his keen attention to detail, and his knowledge of technique and style. Soon little projects turned into big projects for him.

He thrived in Amsterdam, building his collection with love and money. He had an undeniable passion and a steady paycheck. At first he collected drawings and prints then moved on to rare books and many other expressions of art.

The art scene intoxicated him. After work, Emil met with his friends, who were painters, dealers, and collectors. With his carefree spirit and self-absorbed manner, he soon became one of them. In his heart, he was a true bohemian. Emil was handsome at twenty years of age. He had that look and attitude of Rudolf Valentino. He was tall with a body that was lean and solid. His slick brown hair, combed straight back, revealed a sculptured face with intense brown eyes, a perfect straight nose, and a beguiling smile. He oozed charm and walked with an air of confidence and defiance.

When he talked about art, his friends would gather around him, transfixed by his mesmerizing gaze. He craved the attention.

"Let me tell you about the time I dug up a rare pewter vessel beneath a wall of stones," he said. It was one of his childhood adventures of searching for lost treasures at home, just like archaeologists, which he exaggerated with unbelievable suspense and action. He watched to see the look of awe and surprise on their faces.

"More stories!" they cried out, showering Emil with admiration.

He wore a beret cocked over one eye and a colored scarf around his neck, creating a certain charisma. Then he would flash a cocky smile that melted girls' hearts, and his lips pouted with a coy expression to show what he was thinking.

He fit right into Amsterdam's art scene. Each night—over fine Dutch beer and gin that was served with a steaming pot of potatoes, cabbage, sausage, and bacon—he and his friends would discuss art in all its life-forms, including its artists, politics, and society.

Chapter 12

World War II surrounded Emil in 1942. The Netherlands tried to stay neutral when the war broke out in 1939, but its desire for neutrality was ignored. Nazi Germany bombed Rotterdam on May 15, 1940. One day later, the Dutch forces surrendered. The Netherlands was placed under German occupation. The Dutch government fled, and a German civilian governor took over control.

Emil was drafted into the German Army in Amsterdam, but he was no soldier. He was often called into German headquarters for various infractions—never wearing his uniform in public and hanging around with Jews. Many of his closest friends were Jews.

The Germans deported the majority of the Jews to concentration camps with the cooperation of the Dutch police and civil servants. More than half of the Jewish population were killed during the conflict.

The Gestapo questioned and reprimanded Emil on a regular basis. The Gestapo was a secret police organization that used violent methods against people they considered disloyal to Germany. Emil Diesel amused them. He was willful, smart, and always spoke his mind. He took his chances, ignored the threats from the Gestapo, and continued seeing his Jewish friends.

One day, he was pulled into headquarters because he was seen talking to his friend Hans Schulman. He was a dealer of rare old books, master drawings, and prints. They had been friends from the first time Emil arrived in Amsterdam. He introduced Emil to the art community, and with his help, Emil began to build his art collection. It was from

Hans Schulman's shop that he bought his first old master drawing, tribal artifacts, and prints. Emil's interest in rare books grew because of Hans Schulman.

As Emil left the headquarters, he overheard the Gestapo talking. There was to be a raid on Jews the day after tomorrow. He saw Hans across the street and quickly walked over toward him.

"What were you doing over there at headquarters?" Hans asked.

"Hans, can you imagine they told me I could not associate with my friends anymore because they are Jews?"

"I am a Jew," said his friend.

Emil looked around them. He stepped closer and, in a whisper, said, "There is going to be a raid. You had better come to my house. Bring your friends and family."

They all came later that day—Hans, his wife and two children, his parents, a brother, aunts and uncles, and many friends. Emil was surprised but not disturbed to have so many in his small home. He took small trips to the shops for food. Not wanting to look conspicuous, he made sure to go about his duties as usual.

The next day at dusk, the Gestapo, a small handful of them, searched the town's narrow cobblestone streets. The names of Jews were listed in alphabetical order on their lists. They went door to door, knocking at first, then politely forcing their way into homes. They gathered up the Jews and escorted them one by one onto the trucks.

Emil was pleased he could help Hans, his family, and all his friends. He was impressed by their calm, almost stoic manner despite the frightening events all around them. They kept reinforcing positive thoughts of survival. Five days later, it was safe for them to leave. They escaped the Nazi raid and lived through World War II.

Emil was a rebel, and the Gestapo had had enough of his willfulness, but he was valuable to them because of his artistic talent. So the Gestapo had it's army send him to Southern France for a few months then onto the Russian Front. They promoted him to lieutenant because of his education and occupation. One of his jobs was to draw maps so that the officers could plan their strategies, until he became a prisoner of war in Russia.

One eerie and fateful day, Lieutenant Emil, an SS sergeant (elite paramilitary officer of Nazi Germany), and a few soldiers were secured in a bunker on a routine lookout. Russians surrounded them. It was clear that a decision had to be made.

Emil looked at his men. "It's time to surrender. We have a chance to survive."

The SS sergeant was livid. "We are Germans. We don't surrender."

"Bullshit! I am the ranking officer here, and we do what I say. We surrender." Emil had no intention of getting himself killed. He was an artist, not a soldier.

Emil looked at the faces of each enemy soldier glaring down at him in that bunker. He wanted to surrender to the one that looked the most decent—the one who would not shoot. Emil chose a young soldier who looked frail and scared. He waved the flag to him and surrendered. As it turned out, this young Russian was a teacher.

The Russians separated all the prisoners. The SS officer was sent to Siberia in Eastern Russia. Emil remained at the Russian Front in a prisoner-of-war camp. Yet he was placed in a different section of the camp because he was a lieutenant and an artist. It was a lot better there. It was clean, and the treatment wasn't harsh. He found it easy to become friendly with the Russian officers. They could see that he was an artist, not a fanatic Nazi. Emil offered to paint the officers' portraits. They adored the idea because it made them feel important. He used his charm and wit to his advantage, entertaining them with stories of his art adventures. He felt as safe as he could be, considering his circumstances.

He became close with a high-ranking Russian army doctor who worked in the camp. Lydia was beautiful. Short blond curls fell around her face, and her skin was pale from being indoors. Still it gave off a luminescence. Her body was thin but strong underneath her white coat. They became very fond of each other.

He painted her portrait, using long, fluid brushstrokes. She waited for him to caress her with his touch in the same way he caressed her painting with the tip of his brush. He stroked her neck, shoulder, and breasts. She responded to his warm embrace with a passionate kiss. Lust overcame them. She fell in love with Emil, meeting him often in secret so he could finish her portrait. His voracious zest for life captured her heart. His intellect captivated her mind.

The war ended. The German military surrender became effective in Russia on May 9, 1945.

"Emil, there is no future for us, but I want to do something special for you," she said willingly. She had arranged for him to be sent back to Germany. She never saw him again. It was rare for a German prisoner of war to be sent back to Germany.

Germany had been divided into sectors at the end of the war in 1945. Emil did not want to be released to Russian-occupied Germany. He was released instead to a friend in the American sector part of Germany for a short time. He wanted desperately to go back to Amsterdam. He applied for a visa but was denied.

Hans Schulman, his Jewish friend, was shocked to learn Emil was denied entrance into Amsterdam because he was a German officer. Hans and his friends went to the Dutch government and told them their story—how Emil hid them during the raids in Amsterdam and saved them and many other Jews.

In the end, Emil was allowed to return to Amsterdam because he had saved his friends. He reestablished his life there and helped Hans at his shop. Emil became so good at hand coloring that he hand-colored original eighteenth-century black-and-white prints for him. They were as good as the originals and were bought at an even higher price. He was happy and began to collect art again. He never lost sight of his grand plan. He sat with his friends and talked about the days when the art scene was alive.

Emil didn't stay long in Amsterdam. He learned the turmoil in postwar Germany still continued under the new Communist leadership. Erfurt had suffered little damage from the war. The medieval-, baroque-, and classical-style buildings still stood tall.

For a short time after the breakup of Germany on April 12, 1945, American soldiers occupied Erfurt and a small area of land to the Elbe River. The Russians had occupied Berlin, but the Americans wanted a piece of Berlin too. So they gave up Erfurt and the surrounding towns to the Russians to occupy a part of Berlin. The American soldiers left on July 3, 1945. Erfurt was now occupied by the Russians and became part of the German Democratic Republic.

Emil worried that his family was caught up in it all. So in 1946, he left Amsterdam and went back to Erfurt. He gathered all his artwork, antiquities, and all his rare books and prints that had been stored in the American sector of Germany, and he moved back home to stay.

Chapter 13

Emil met Zelda Kaiser in Erfurt in the midsummer of 1946. She was twenty years old. Emil was thirty-six. She was stunning—slim, sexy, and bright—and she knew it. She had raven-black hair and deep-blue eyes. Her beauty fascinated him like a fine illustration on canvas. From that moment, he had to have her.

Zelda lived in one of the neighborhoods near his house. He remembered walking by her street many times when she was a young child and seeing her play in the sandbox. Now she was all grown up. How fortuitous for him. He decided she had all the right ingredients to make a fine wife.

In Erfurt, from 1933 to 1945, the children had to learn English in school. Zelda was quick to learn English and spoke it quite well. She wasn't a serious student, but she did enjoy singing at the local opera house and at private events. She even asked her father to send her to school to study opera.

The American officers invited her to all their parties. The soldiers loved to shower this raving beauty with attention, especially when she spoke English to them with her low, sultry voice. She was their movie star.

In 1945, Zelda had been dating an American soldier, and in early spring, she had a child—Marie. He was falling in love with Zelda, and he wanted to take her and their daughter to the States with him. She refused to go. She couldn't imagine leaving her father, who had always spoiled her and still took care of her. She was her father's special girl.

Her American officer went back to the States, and she raised Marie on her own. When Zelda was not singing, she helped her father in his wholesale business. He sold equipment and supplies to most of the hotels and restaurants in the area.

This life was not exciting enough for her. Then she met Emil Diesel. They were relentless in their pursuit of each other, and they fell madly in love.

"I want you," he said.

"I need you," she said.

This handsome man was smart and stable, and he did not care that she had a young child. Zelda and Emil were so much alike; they made a great pair. They married six months later in Erfurt, on December 10, 1946.

They moved to the second floor of her parents' house. Emil, Zelda, and little Marie settled in with nannies and a housekeeper. Two years later, in April, Maximilian was born. Emil was proud to have a son.

After the war, in the early fifties, Zelda's father divorced her mother and left for the West. Zelda's mother, Gunda, moved downstairs with Zelda's brother, Jurgen, his wife, and daughter, Marlene. Gunda passed away soon after.

At the same time, Karla, Emil's sister, moved to West Germany with her husband, a police officer. Emil did not think much of his sister, complaining she was a stupid, silly girl and would never do anything productive with her life. Karla was happy to move to the West for good.

In the late fifties, Emil's father left for the West after his divorce too. His mother, Frieda, came to live with them on the second floor. They were forced to rent the third and fourth floors to strangers.

Under the new East German law, every family was allowed to have only so much space to live in—a certain number of meters per family. Each floor was partitioned off. Emil's family had several rooms throughout the second floor and had to share their space with strangers brought in by the Communists. He was concerned for his family. It was not easy for them to share their house with strangers. Emil was suspicious of his tenants.

His tenants, who were a quiet couple, moved into the rooms that were partitioned off from the Diesel apartment. He might have been a military officer or a Stasi agent. Emil and Zelda noticed he had a bust of Stalin in his living room, like a shrine. Once Stalin was no longer popular anymore and was declared a criminal according to the Communists, he put it away. Despite being a Prussian Communist, he and his wife were always polite to Emil and his family, though they kept to themselves.

For a while, many of Emil's friends thought he was a Communist. This tenant had placed the red, black, and gold striped flag of East Germany outside by the front steps. His friends walked by his house, shaking their heads in dismay.

"Can you believe that Emil has become a member?" Later, they discovered Emil had to take in tenants under the authority of the East German regime.

For three years, Emil worked as a graphic illustrator for a small publishing company. Outside of work, he collected art as much as he could and spent less time with his son. Zelda looked for small singing jobs, and the nannies were busy taking care of Max and Marie. Her mother never could accept Marie. She fought for attention any way she could. Marie became insolent and often disobeyed. Her mother did not know how to handle her. As Marie got older, she was sent away to school or to relatives. Max had his own insecurities to deal with concerning his family and didn't remember Marie much growing up. She was mostly out, not in, his life.

Emil and Zelda entertained at home. Their guests were close friends, usually art lovers and musicians. They filled their living room with laughter and song—a cigarette in one hand and a drink in the other.

One time, Emil's friends were in deep discussions about the art world. Everyone smoked. Smoke filled the room so fast it blocked the light coming from the windows. It seeped under the doorway and out into the street. The smoke was so bad a passerby thought the house was on fire. The fire truck came. Emil opened the door and assured the firefighters there was no fire. It was just smoke from their cigarettes.

Emil decided to work on his own. It was time. He got an exclusive job freelancing for the Linden East German Advertising Agency, a government agency. He was given privileges because only a handful of people did this type of work. The best privilege was, they allowed him to work at home. He loved his job and worked quickly. Each week, he finished his work for the agency faster than the estimated time the government said the work would take to get done. This gave him more time to search for art.

Often, little Max would wake up in the middle of the night. He would tiptoe in bare feet down the back stairs, through the kitchen, and to the library. And he would watch Emil work from behind the half-open door. His father was so engrossed in his work he did not notice him. Poor Max wondered if his father would ever have time for him.

Emil worked fast and smart. He delivered his work every Friday on time, and he never told them he had finished it on Tuesday. His work always pleased them, and that was why he was paid very well. All that free time gave Emil the opportunity to concentrate on building his art collection. He attended all the auctions he could find and sought out the estates and castles of aristocrats.

Chapter 14

Throughout the area, the East Germans confiscated estates and castles. The aristocrats, the owners or heirs, could only live in a few rooms in their own castle or estate. They kept a few belongings, including their art. The Communist government placed tenants— strangers—in other rooms. They did not believe any one family needed so much space to live in. Older aristocrats were given a small pension.

Emil went to these castles and estates to buy the aristocrats' art. They were selling their art so they could have enough money to sustain themselves because their pensions were not enough. Only the older parents and family members remained, and many were widows. Their children were fleeing to the West. People wanted to sell their art to Emil because he paid them more money for their art than what the government art galleries would pay. Word spread that Emil gave a good price for art. People sought him out, often arriving at his door to sell their art.

It didn't take him long to acquire an incredible amount of art.

He collected all kinds of art: Egyptian and Etruscan art from ancient Etruria; Roman sculptures of heads, hands, and other body parts; German porcelain figurines; Renaissance silver and coins; Gothic statues and medieval art; old master drawings; and religious paintings. All this had passed down through generations.

Collecting became an obsession.

There was quite a bit of activity at his house—people coming and going—that Emil was unaware the Stasi were watching him from an apartment they had rented in a house across the street. Binoculars peeked, cameras clicked, and notes were scribbled.

During the late forties and fifties, the Russians did not patrol the borders often. There were no minefields or barbed wire fences separating the land between East Germany and West Germany. Emil thought hard. He did not want to lose his connections in the West.

He knew of a train that carried passengers from a small town near the border of East Germany and West Germany to another town near the border. The train traveled on tracks that went through West German land for a short distance before entering East Germany again. Only people living in the proximity of the town could get special tickets to travel by this train to the other town.

Emil knew what these tickets looked like, and he duplicated the original ticket. He was good at forging the tickets and using them to get on the train. He knew from the train schedule when the train left the station, at what point the train entered West Germany and then East Germany again, and when it arrived at the next station. This old train moved over rolling hills and valleys at a very slow speed.

Emil took the train by himself. When the train arrived at the point where it passed through West German soil, Emil would jump from the train. A car would wait for him there. He would visit his friends who were collectors. At the local coffee house with his friends, he read the Western newspapers over coffee and then exchanged stories over beer about what was happening in their own lives. They were different worlds—the East and the West. Some stories were filled with laughter, some with tears.

He missed the art world outside the East and was excited to learn what was bought and sold at auctions and which artists were in or out. He was in the West for a few hours each time. He knew when the last train was returning to the town in the East. He had his friend drive him to the drop-off point, then he would jump back onto the slow-moving train and ride the train back to the station.

Each time, his friend would say, "Why don't you stay for good? Bring your family over and make a life here."

Each time he would shake his head and smile. "I can't. I must return to my art. It is where I belong."

It wasn't long before the Russians tightened the borders and put up the barbed wire fences. Looking back, he thought, *was a good run!*

Chapter 15

In the early fifties, Zelda's father, who had been divorced from his wife for many years, decided to move to the West, to the quaint resort town of Garmisch, nestled among the Bavarian Alps along the Bavarian Road. He set up a small wholesale restaurant supply and hotel equipment business as he had done in Erfurt. He was quite a womanizer, as was Emil's father.

In Garmisch, he met a twenty-year-old girl. He married her and had a child with her. Soon after, she took off with a US soldier and their child. She divorced him. He realized nothing much ever changed in life, and he vowed never to do it again.

Often, Zelda took Max and Marie to visit her father in Garmisch. Each time, the East Germans gave her an exit visa for four weeks. The last time, she stayed for six months. Zelda wanted to find work.

"There is an American intelligence officer living in a big villa with his wife and two girls," said her father. "They are looking for a nanny and a housekeeper for the children."

Zelda pouted as she looked over their offer. "I don't know. It's not the kind of work I expected to do, but the pay is good."

She thought back to all those times Emil had left them to search for more precious possessions and how he had forgotten to leave them some household money to buy food and staples for the family. She would have to take merchandise from her father's wholesale business to sell or barter just to have enough money to pay for coal for the furnace. If she took this job, she would have her own money.

Zelda was young, confident, and stylish. Her English was perfect. She moved into the villa only with Max, leaving Marie with her father. Marie was older than Max, and Zelda felt she could help her grandfather with his work. But the truth was, she did not want her.

The American officer and his wife welcomed Zelda and Max into their family. They adored Max and loved having a little six-year-old boy around. If Zelda reprimanded Max for his behavior, the couple defended him. He was learning English. As they prepared to leave for the States, they asked if they could take Max with them. Zelda refused, of course, but did not get annoyed about it. She liked the money too much.

While Zelda and the children were living in Garmisch, Emil was living at home alone. One evening, he entertained their good friend Deirdre, who was an actress in the theatre. She was blonde, curvaceous, and could wile any man. Not only did she keep Emil company, she maneuvered her way into his bed, paying no mind to her friend Zelda. Emil had a tumultuous affair with her, unbeknownst to his wife. At the same time, Zelda thought it was kind of Deirdre to visit Emil while she was away. The thought of Emil cheating on her never entered her mind.

When Zelda returned home and saw Deirdre living with Emil in her house, she cried, "Divorce!" Deirdre moved out right away. Emil tried to appease Zelda.

"I'm sorry. I was stupid," he said.

"I don't care." She could only think of herself and how hurt she was.

Zelda reacted in haste. In 1954, the divorce papers were filed. They got their divorce. Walking out of the court, they both had regrets. Tears fell. They wrapped their arms around each other, realizing they had made a terrible mistake.

Zelda sobbed. "We should have listened to each other."

"I know. It was my fault," he said.

"Emil, I should have never been gone so long."

They did not want to believe they were divorced, but the papers made it final.

They decided to ignore the divorce papers and pretend it never happened. They never told anyone what they had done. In their own eyes, they were still married. As the years went by, the divorce was forgotten. Life went on as usual.

Chapter 16

Emil collected his art, and Zelda went about her daily routine. Everything appeared to be fine. On occasion, Zelda visited her sister, Arianna, in the West. She was married to a doctor who worked at the American hospital as a civilian. Zelda was a beautiful magnet for attention. A week after her return home, she was picked up and questioned by the KGB, the Russian secret police, because she had been in the West with her sister and her husband.

They interrogated her and, to her amazement, offered her a job. They wanted her to spy on the American doctor and find out what was going on in the West. When Emil found out that Zelda was detained and questioned by the KGB, he made a big scene, carrying on how they could question his wife, an innocent woman who was just visiting her sister, and he told them that he had friends in high places. They let her go. She was relieved. She had no intention of working for the Russians as a spy.

In 1960, Zelda took Max and Marie and moved to West Germany without Emil. They moved to the outskirts of the city of Düsseldorf to live with her father. Again, he had married and moved into his wife's estate. Zelda's doting father bought her a condominium in Düsseldorf and provided her with a monthly allowance for life. He set her up in her own business, selling entertainment equipment such as jukeboxes.

It was not the hard economic times in East Germany or the lack of freedom under the GDR that motivated Zelda to leave Emil behind. It was far worse. It was her niece, Marlene, her brother's daughter. Marlene was gorgeous and sexy with wavy blond hair that cascaded down her back and deep ice-blue eyes that could weaken even the strongest man. She was eighteen years old. Emil was forty-nine.

Zelda was close to her niece. For many years, they lived one floor from each other. Marlene had spent much of her time upstairs. They were all family. Emil and Marlene became close. She would spend afternoons with him, talking about her ballet dancing, and he talked to her about his adventures collecting art. As she grew older, she took a serious interest in the restoration of art, drawing them closer together. Zelda was happiest when Emil was working and not around the house, because there was no Marlene either. She was getting tired of listening to the two of them carry on about art.

It was inevitable. The affair began. Zelda discovered them together one night. She saw them in his room, on his bed, kissing and groping each other. She looked at Marlene in disgust. Marlene told her the affair had been going on for months.

"I am leaving you for good," Zelda said.

Her eyes burned a hole in his heart.

This affair was not the only reason why Zelda moved to the West. Lately, he was asking too much of her. For Emil, it was always about his precious possessions. She could never forget how Emil forced her to sleep with his friend Muller. He was an antique dealer who had a seventeenth-century painting that Emil wanted very much. Emil noticed that Muller was attracted to his beautiful wife, Zelda.

"Zelda, you must go out with him. I want you to get me that painting, even if you have to sleep with him—whatever it takes."

She could not find a way to change his mind. To be fair, Zelda continued sleeping with Muller. She used him when she wanted to have sex since she was not getting any sex at home with Emil. Preoccupied with her own needs, she ignored the signs that led up to the affair with Marlene.

Getting out of the East was not as easy as Zelda thought. She needed to pass through East Berlin because East Germany's borders were closed. She did not tell Max and Marie they were leaving for good.

"Max, bring your stamp collection," she said.

He agreed, but he thought it was odd that he needed to take his stamps.

First, they went to Potsdam to meet their contact, Wilhelm Voigt, a friend of Emil's who was an important person in the Communist Party. The border guards made spot checks at the subway station where they would check papers of those passengers going to West Berlin. Voigt walked with them as they passed by the border guards. They were not stopped. The guards acknowledged Voigt and turned away.

Zelda, Max, and Marie boarded the subway headed for West Berlin. On the busy main shopping street, Kurfürstendamm, in an apartment overlooking the shops, Zelda and her children stayed two days with mutual friends of hers and Emil's. Many times throughout the years, they had helped Emil store his art.

From West Berlin, they flew to Hanover. Zelda's sister and her husband picked them up at the airport. Every person who left the East to live permanently in the West must pass through immigration. Zelda gave the officer her papers and the children's papers. The officer read that she had an American child, Marie. He pulled her aside. She spoke impeccable English to them. They were quite impressed with her and asked her if she wanted to work for the CIA—to spy on the East Germans. Of course, to do this, she would have to go back to live in East Germany.

"No, thank you. I prefer to go to the West." She flashed them a big smile, adding, "It is amusing. The East Germans asked me to spy on you too. I also declined them."

"No kidding." They all had a chuckle over that. They didn't pressure her. Two days later, Zelda, Max, and Marie took a plane to Düsseldorf.

Emil had showed up the day after they arrived in West Berlin. He thought his wife was bluffing. He begged her to come back to Erfurt.

"I am finished with Marlene. Please don't go. Come back," he said.

"I can't," she said. She believed he loved her, and she did love him.

"I will not leave, Zelda. You will have to leave me." Emil sulked like a defeated little boy.

She stood her ground for the first time. "Enough! I'm leaving," she said. "You can never change. You will never change."

"Don't go back." Twelve-year-old Max pleaded with his mother. He remembered how bad his father had treated him. He never forgot the harsh scolding from his father when he was caught being idle. Either he was sent to his room to read and draw, or he was asked to write on the chalkboard one hundred times "I will behave". He wanted to live in the West.

Hearing this, Emil's eyes filled with tears. Emil could not believe Max wanted to go to the West with his mother and leave him behind.

Emil knew he could not join them in the West. He had to stay with his art in the East. Zelda knew she never would return to the East.

He was stunned. He could not believe what just happened. He left the apartment in despair, his head tucked into his chest.

Zelda walked away with the children, leaving him all alone.

Chapter 17

Emil returned to Erfurt and withdrew to the confinement of his home. He missed Zelda and the children. How could he let it get so out of control? His recklessness was his fault. He should have paid more attention to Zelda and Max. He was guilty.

Alas, he could not help himself; he was a weak man. He could not resist Marlene. He craved the attention of this beautiful young woman and took her. And she was ready to be taken. He devoured her with desire and lust. She seduced him in the morning as the sun was rising and in the darkest hours of the night.

At breakfast, she sat across from him, her eyes focused on his. She broke off a piece from the dark fibrous bread then slowly spread a thin layer of butter and sweet lingonberry jam. Her mouth took it whole. She pressed her lips together, chewing in slow motion, her deep-blue eyes still focused on his. She could sense how aroused he was. He wanted her right there on the table.

He tried not to think about her during the day, but he couldn't concentrate. His beautiful distraction often cost him a purchase at an auction. Each item he chose seemed to have her imprint on it. Marlene had become an obsession, just like one of his pieces of art.

That evening, Marlene sat by the fire in the tapestry-covered chair, her long legs crossed while she was sipping straight vodka like fine wine. Emil sat across from her. She listened to him talk about his latest acquisitions. Her seductive eyes and wanting mouth excited him and drove him crazy. He couldn't take his eyes off hers. He reached down beside his chair, his hand probing the floor until he felt the coolness of the object. He raised it high, presenting a pewter chalice to her as if he were standing on the church altar.

She clapped her hands with delight. "Wonderful! Tell me more."

"The chalice was brought to me by a young man who returned from the war. After researching it, I found out who the original owners were and where it came from. The chalice came from a small German church in eastern Prussia, which was part of Poland. It is dated 1665. See, right here, the name of the priest—Joseph Ghent—is engraved on it. Maybe a soldier took it during the war. Look, it still has a patina." He pointed as he spoke. "The wide mouth of the chalice is worn. It must have been used during the communion rites. The solid base of the chalice is carved with circular rings. Its middle is thick and was made this way so that it could be held. The base has a four-lined pi detail around it. It must have been left behind at the altar because it was probably used daily by the priests."

As he saw Marlene's eyes light up with joy, he could feel the excitement run through his body. Zelda was never interested in art the way Marlene was. That was a shame. Maybe it could have saved their marriage.

Marlene studied art restoration at school, and many nights she came home late. Emil watched the clock. The more time passed, the more impatient he grew, suspicious that she was meeting another man younger than him. He did not want to think about her clandestine affairs as long as she came home.

Strolling in, Marlene flung her arms around Emil and kissed him hard on the mouth. "I'm sorry I'm so late again."

"It's all right," he said in a sullen voice.

Emil reached out, took her by the hand, and led her into the bedroom down the narrow hall. The bed was small, and thick sheets covered the mattress. Turning down the warm, soft, down comforter, they slid under the blanket. Their bodies touched. With his strong arms, he lifted his body carefully on top of her. He was wild with passion. He kissed her mouth and breasts,. He was aware of the heat moving up his lower loins, of the sweat building at his neck. He felt the flush in his face and the rush of blood to his head. Turning onto his back, his entire body exhausted, he collapsed.

His heart beating fast, he thought, *I wish it could have been like this with Zelda?* Thankful Marlene was in his life at all, he did not care if she was sleeping with others.

In the end, he knew he would always have his art to comfort him.

Chapter 18

Since 1949, both the Federal Republic of Germany and the German Democratic Republic had established themselves as two separate states and Berlin as two separate cities. The federal republic perceived Berlin as a federal state, and the GDR claimed Berlin as the capital of the democratic republic.

By 1953, competition in East Berlin and West Berlin was fierce. Western ideas through weekly broadcasts spilled into the East, causing political and social unrest. Mass protests over low wages and high prices caused the government to ban meetings and impose curfews. Demands grew for the removal of quotas and free elections. Over two hundred thousand people from the GDR fled to the West, causing a temporary closing of the inner-city border of Berlin. But the exodus still continued.

In 1956, the Soviet premier Nikita Khrushchev said that Berlin would be the place where the East-West confrontation would take place. "An ideological war will not only be fought there, but also an economic war between socialism and capitalism. The outcome," he said, "would be determined by which regime had created better material conditions."

In 1958, Khrushchev demanded the whole of Berlin become a part of the GDR. This meant the withdrawal of the Western Allies and the transformation of Berlin into a free city. The Allies feared the GDR would impose a complete blockade around West Berlin. They rejected the ultimatum with no immediate consequences.

The East's government had tried to establish its own identity, but it was falling behind the West economically, especially in Berlin. Their citizens were crossing into West Berlin to live and work, which made the East lose its population.

In September 1960, Walter Ulbricht became head of the GDR and decided to order the construction of a wall separating East Berlin and West Berlin. In August 1961, Erich Honecker carried out Ulbricht's orders to build the Berlin Wall. The construction of the Berlin Wall began, first with barbed wire fences and then eventually replaced by concrete border installations, which prevented anyone from escaping.

This was done even though two months before the wall went up, Ulbricht had said, "No one has any intention of building a wall."

On August 13, 1961, East Berlin began to be sealed off from the West. The GDR closed the inner German border. The wall was meant to provide economic stability and the consolidation of East Germany by preventing the escape of the masses into West Germany. In 1971, Erich Honecker replaced Walter Ulbricht.

Emil continued to buy art from the aristocrats who needed money more than ever to live. Supplies of food and goods were scarce. Desperate people came with one piece of art a week to sell to Emil. He never turned anyone away, no matter if the piece was of value or not. He knew they needed to survive. He continued building an extensive art collection. He didn't let the turmoil and upheaval around him disrupt his search for more artwork. It was unbelievable; the closed borders had helped him by reducing competition.

It had become impossible to cross the border at restricted checkpoints through West Berlin. The strained relations between the East and the West caused problems. Increasing controls by the state were placed on television, radio, and international calls. The censorship of artists and writers forced them to move outside Berlin. Everything seemed to be monitored and watched.

Emil watched his back as well. For years, he noticed black cars with darkened windows parked across the street from his home at various times during the day. It was obvious that they were watching him come and go from the house. Yet they never crossed the street. He was amused, laughing at their boldness. He mumbled, "The Stasi must think I am stupid."

"I have nothing to hide and have done nothing wrong," he said to his friends. His strong, well-established ego, exuberance, and integrity kept him fearless, but did it keep him safe?

Chapter 19

In Erfurt, Emil kept only a small circle of friends. They gathered at his house and discussed their colorful pasts over drinks.

He rose from his chair, raising his glass to them. "I have realized a true art collector's life is to live passionately through his art."

They raised their glasses. "To Emil."

Into the night they laughed, drank, and talked about their adventures. It was Emil who had the best and the most colorful adventures.

"I loved living in Amsterdam as a young man. The city was bursting with rebirth. There wasn't a day I didn't walk through the Museumplein [Museum Square] on the way to my favorite museum, the Rijksmuseum, which opened in 1885. I would spend hours gazing at the collections of Rembrandt and Vermeer. The Van Gogh Museum took my breath away, but it was the Stedelijk, a museum of modern art [1895], that caused me to shift my perception of the abstract in a new way.

"Commerce was booming along the Amsterdam–Rhine Canal and the North Sea Canal. It was the thirties, and everything—the music, fashion design, and movies—was provocative. Life was happening! That's why they called this era Amsterdam's second golden age."

Emil was a relentless prankster. He told the story about one visit with his mother in Erfurt. "I brought with me a beautiful Dutch Indonesian girl. Her coal-black hair fell like silk down her back to the edge of her spine. Her body moved like a gazelle. Her sultry dark eyes stole glances from me the whole time. My mother was frantic. I knew that she was praying that this girl was not engaged to her fine German son. I must tell you her prayers were answered. It was just a visit." Emil enjoyed taunting his mother because it was so easy to do.

"Often I sent pictures home to my mother to show her my experiences and what life was like there. This is one of the pictures showing me sitting in a wide tufted high-back chair. This is my friend sitting close to me on the arm of the chair. His arm is around me, hugging my shoulders. Both of us are looking down at the pages of a book. Puzzled, my mother had said, 'Who is that boy?' 'He is my dear errand boy,' I had said to her."

His friends looked at the picture then grinned at Emil. His mother truly believed he was his errand boy. They all knew who he really was—a very close friend.

Emil discovered that living with various artists in the art community was exciting and stimulating. Once, he lived with a photographer named Harley. He accompanied him on photo shoots to learn how he expressed art through photography. Emil admired his talent, as well as Harley's own physical form. He was gorgeous. His warm brown skin glistened in the light. His muscular body showed his strength and vitality. They were both in their twenties—young and reckless. Emil was charming and adventurous; Harley, creative and sensitive. They explored the art scene together with a zealous pursuit of passion. Through Harley's many photographs of the nude form, Emil acquired a new appreciation of the nude form as art.

African tribal art was popular then. Emil and Harley embraced the trend. In Amsterdam, there was a large population of Asian and African immigrants from the Dutch colonies during the seventeenth and eighteenth century.

They brought with them African masks, carved totem poles, and small wooden ceremonial figures to sell. One very rare figure had thick nails stuck into its body; it was called a ceremonial fetish, which was sought after by collectors and museums.

His friends raised their glasses to Emil's impetuous nature, amused—but not without a little envy in their hearts.

Emil's life in Amsterdam gave him the opportunity to fulfill his dream—not just to be an artist, but also to become an important collector of his time. One experience took him to Egypt on an archaeological dig. Harley worked freelance for various magazines, similar to *National Geographic*. He had to photograph an important archaeological dig in Luxor, the site of the ancient city of Thebes. He asked Emil to join him on the dig. Emil was elated.

It was a wild adventure. They joined another group at the site and were driven in open vehicles out to the dig site. They slaved under the hot sun for hours, looking for ancient relics. Emil found several artifacts on his own, such as small stone jars and pieces of broken statues. He could not stop talking about his discoveries.

The Egyptian government was not interested in providing monetary support for their museum's archaeological digs. However, they were pleased the Germans, Dutch, and British came with their shovels and did the work for them.

The archaeologists shared their discoveries from the dig with the Egyptian museums. This did not matter to Emil. The incredible experience in Egypt drove him to become an important collector of Egyptian art. Emil brought back Egyptian figures, jewelry, and small pieces of pottery. He thanked Harley from his heart for giving him the best time of his life.

Emil's reputation grew. He was now considered a collector and expert, especially of Chinese art and antiquities. The director of the Asian museum in Berlin chose Emil to join the museum as a consultant on early Chinese art. He was asked to be part of an archaeological expedition to dig in China. The director gave him an important status—as the official expert on early Chinese art—because he could detect early Chinese artifacts without needing a test to confirm his findings. Emil was that good.

His friends had to leave before curfew. Each day followed into the next day. Emil thrived alone in the little world he created for himself. He spent hours looking through books and searching through the pages until he was able to solve the mystery of a particular piece of art. He believed each piece held clues to its beginnings and its owners. For hours, he sat at his desk, scrutinizing one symbol or signature with his magnifying glass on a hand-painted miniature. His research was impeccable. He could tell the age of an artifact just by looking at it. He knew he was better than any curator in the Gera Museum.

Alone in his home, his thoughts drifted to his Sunday excursions to the museum with Max. He had hoped Max would follow in his footsteps—that is, to love art as much he did. He missed his boy. How could Max leave him? He sat motionless in his worn Gothic chair, his head cocked to one side as his hand rested underneath his chin. So much despair for one person to take.

He was desperate, saying with utmost certainty, "One day I will have my own museum. It will be my greatest achievement. Max will be proud of me."

Chapter 20

It was 1960. Zelda settled into her apartment in Düsseldorf with twelve-year-old Max and fourteen-year-old Marie. She was happy to have the concession business her father had given her. The jukeboxes were popular in the small diners and cafes. She collected money from them twice a week.

Max and Marie adjusted to their new school. German and English were spoken, no Russian. Both were confident and outspoken. They didn't have any trouble making friends. Max had quite an ego for a young man; he thought he knew everything. His studies were easy, so he got bored quickly. This led to his mischievous behavior. Joking with the other kids got him into trouble, and he started skipping classes, though he always kept up with his studies.

He was a smart and lucky boy. Max could pass his final exams without much effort, whereas others worked very hard to achieve good grades.

His teacher took him aside later. "Max, you are a very intelligent boy, and you are so fortunate that everything comes easy to you. Yet you choose to go by the path of least resistance. If you applied yourself more, you could accomplish great things."

"I will try," he said, giving it only a brief moment of thought.

It was no wonder that he was so industrious at a young age. Max liked to work and have money in his pocket. He worked odd jobs all through his years at school. He delivered newspapers, groceries, and laundry. He gave out fliers for advertising and worked setting up candlepins at a bowling alley. At Christmas, he bought bags full of used stamps from all over the word. He steamed them off the envelopes and pasted them onto pages in a book and sold them. He made more money on Christmas and was able to buy gifts for his mother and sister.

School was the natural course for a well-bred German boy. At the university in Düsseldorf, he studied engineering while apprenticing. When he chose engineering as his career, all he got was grief from his mother.

"How could you choose a blue-collar job and not the arts? You will be on a treadmill for life."

In between, he served eighteen months in the army. He finished his studies in 1969.

For six months, in 1965, Max corresponded with a girl student from the United States whom he had met in Germany. Helga was born in Hamburg and had moved with her parents to New York in the early sixties. After her studies, she became a stewardess and flew from Boston to Düsseldorf. Max acquired a visiting visa for six months and flew to the city of Boston, where she had to relocate for work. He saw her often.

Max could not get Helga out his mind. She was lovely and had a pleasant demeanor. He loved her independence and undaunted nature. She was right for him. Helga fell for his charm and good looks. He made her laugh. She liked that he was as independent as her. Flying back and forth was not working for him; he wanted to be with her. In 1970, they decided to marry. Before he made the move to the United States permanent, he had to see his father in East Germany.

Through the years, Max's relationship with his father remained distant and cold. From 1960 to 1970, he had not seen or talked to his father. Yet every year, Max had received a card from him on Christmas and one on his birthday.

At his wedding, Aunt Karla had taken him aside. "You must go to see your father before you leave. He has a huge art collection. You need to know what is going on there, Max. You are the only heir."

"I'm not sure if I should go. He doesn't care."

Max realized that he had made a big mistake not keeping in contact with his father. He considered his Aunt Karla's advice—he had to see his father.

Max's mother did not want him to go. She was afraid that if Max crossed into East Germany, he would not be able to come back.

In September 1970, with mixed emotions, Max planned to meet his father in East Berlin before he and his wife left for the States. He had to know if his father cared about him enough to let him into his life. He also had to confront his own feelings about his father. He had to find out for himself what he had missed. He sent a telegram to his father that he wanted to see him.

He flew to Tempelhof Airport along with his new wife. Armed guards watched their every move. They dared not speak or look around them. With checked papers in hand, they passed through Checkpoint Charlie, the crossing point between East and West Berlin. His father and Marlene were waiting on the other side on Friedrichstraß.

Emil waved to Max first. Max rushed toward him. Tears fell. They hugged for a long time.

"I have missed you, Max."

"Father, if I knew that, I would have come sooner. All I got from you were cards in the mail."

Emil felt Max's pain like a sharp blade to the heart.

"Father, I missed you."

Max saw Marlene standing next to Emil. He hesitated as he kissed his cousin on the cheek. He had heard the rumors about Marlene and his father, but he decided he did not want to embarrass her. He didn't care about her. He was there only for his father.

Emil handed a gift to Max. It was a small carved Buddha and three woodblock prints. Max choked up; his father had never given him a gift. He did not know what to say to him except "Thank you."

Their pass allowed them only a few hours. They did not have much time to talk. They lunched at a café near the checkpoint, trying to catch up on the ten years they had missed.

It was a cold, gray, and misty day. They could hear the trains passing overhead. Old glass lampposts lined each cement sidewalk for blocks.

They talked about everyday life and caught up on the past, such as Max's education and work.

They had no time alone to talk about art. His father had so much to tell him, and Max needed to know. Helga and Marlene sat quietly, fading into the background. When it was time to leave, their farewells were difficult to comprehend. Too much time had passed.

All they could say to each other was "See you soon."

Max had to leave the Buddha behind, but the three woodblock prints were rolled up and hidden under his wife's mink coat. When they crossed back into the West, the border guard checked only her identity card because she was American. By then, visiting privileges had eased up at the border on the Communist side. Max looked back at his father with tears of regret—a feeling that he had never experienced. An anguished Emil watched as Max crossed into another life.

Chapter 21

Throughout the '60s and into the early '70s, the Stasi watched Emil come and go, but they did nothing. They wanted information. They built a surveillance file, accumulating thousands of pages of paper on the graphic designer. They put together a large network around him of informers: friends, business associates, his contacts, and maybe some family members. The Stasi realized he was well respected in the community and at his work at the Linden East German Advertising Agency. He was valuable to the state because of his expertise in his job. The Stasi knew Emil Diesel was not a Communist Party member, and because of this, he was considered an enemy of the state.

The Stasi approached the people who knew Emil. They conspired, through intimidation and threats, to persuade them to spy on him. The tenants who lived on the second floor watched Emil and reported to the Stasi. Even Emil's trusted chauffeur and caretaker was asked to inform about Emil's whereabouts. One by one, they brought them into the network. In the end, they ended up spying on one another.

Emil depended on Gustav to take him wherever he wanted to go since he never learned to drive. He was too busy and impatient when he was young to learn.

Gustav drove him to the countryside of Erfurt to visit the estates. He liked Emil because he treated him well. He gave him a good salary with benefits and provided him with groceries that were hard to find. There was loyalty between them. Gustav fulfilled his obligations to the Stasi and turned in his notebook every week, although he made up most of the information he put in the book. Gustav's wife was an informer too. She watched her husband.

One Saturday, Emil told Gustav to get the car ready because they were traveling to Weimar. His mother packed them a lunch and plenty of water. Gustav drove through the rolling hills of the Thuringian Forest, passing red-roofed villages along the way. Weimar was the home of the famous poet Johann Wolfgang von Goethe, the famous composers Franz Liszt and Richard Strauss, and the philosopher Friedrich Nietzsche. Often Emil enjoyed strolling along the wide boulevards and through its beautiful parks. The city attracted a cultural and artistic crowd because of its famous past.

Emil sat in the back seat of his car. It was so quiet he could hear the humming sound of the tires. As his eyes shifted from one side of the road to the other, he marveled at the muted colors of the forest filtered by the sunlight. His noticed a black car following four car lengths behind them. He wondered how long the car would follow them.

Emil wore a smirk on his lips as he glanced behind him again. The black car was still there. He noticed Gustav never mentioned the car and kept his eyes on the road.

"Sir, are we staying long?"

"No more than two hours."

Emil pulled out of his pocket a small wood figure no bigger than four inches tall, carved in the shape on an old Chinese man. It had two strands of beard that hung low to his chest. One hand held a small round object, possibly a piece of fruit. The other hand held a staff, a walking stick. It was a very fine piece from the sixteenth century that looked like new.

Gustav entered the city of Weimar. Emil glanced back. He noticed the car was still following them. Emil leaned over the front seat, pointing to the narrow cobblestone street on their right. "Gustav, park in front of the store. Wait here."

He surveyed the area before closing the car door behind him, seeing nothing unusual. He snuck behind the shop and checked the back alley and the side streets. There were no sinister characters lurking about yet. He took a deep breath and calmly walked into the store. It was filled with antiques. His friend, Thomas, greeted him with a big hug, a huge smile, and a cup of coffee.

Emil had conducted business with Thomas in the past. They sipped coffee, and Emil took the wood figure out of his pocket. Thomas grinned when he saw it. He shook hands with Emil. Thomas went to the back of his store and brought Emil two hand-cut wine glasses with the initial *M* carved in the middle. He presented them to Emil.

"These are the court wine glasses made for Marie Antoinette."

He placed one in his hand. Emil felt the weight and looked at the clarity of the glass. The base and stem was thick and sturdy, not delicate—a glass used every day. He studied the diamond-patterned band around each glass and the small emblem with the initial *M*. Smiling with pleasure, Emil patted Thomas on the back. The trade was complete.

He left the store with the glasses tucked into each pocket, knowing that the Stasi would soon acquire another person in their network, but they cannot prove that any crime was committed. Emil laughed at the ridiculousness of the Stasi, as if they had nothing better to do than follow him around. He hoped they enjoyed the ride. All the way home, Emil sat back and let his body relax. Closing his eyes, he imagined himself at court, sipping fine wine from the glasses with Marie Antoinette. Little did he realize, Gustav had written down the encounter for the Stasi to see.

Later that year, Emil heard about the demise of one of his dear friends. He was a surgeon who collected beautiful paintings. He tried to smuggle a painting out of East Germany. They caught him at the border with the painting rolled up inside the long handle of his umbrella.

He never knew his wife was the informer. He was picked up and put in jail. She watched him to see who his contact was and informed the police when he left the house that day. Their marriage was in trouble. She had filed for divorce—that was his mistake.

He became a prisoner of exchange—a common practice between the East and the West. His devious wife was left with his art collection. Emil thought it was a tragic story because he lost his collection.

Chapter 22

Each piece of art has a story behind its provenance. Investigating the history of an art piece was Emil's greatest pleasure. An incredible piece of furniture had fallen into his hands. The story behind the piece was most fascinating.

In 1968, Emil acquired a pristine German pine chest painted in chinoiserie style. Its Chinese qualities were reflected in the relief of colorful motifs. He bought it from his friend Muller's father, who was also an antique dealer in Erfurt. The dealer bought it from a dealer from the town of Menning. This antique dealer acquired it from a baron who lived in a castle outside the same town.

The baron was a highly decorated colonel in World War II. He wanted to sell the cabinet and give the money to a young woman whom he got pregnant. The sale almost did not happen. The Russian authorities came to the castle, hunting for valuables. They approached the cabinet and pulled at the door handles to open the cabinet and drawers in the middle of the chest. They pulled so hard they broke the handle on one of the drawers. In disgust, they left the chest and continued to look around. The baron was relieved. He did not want the Russians to remove the piece from the castle. He sold the cabinet to the antique dealer in Menning and sent the woman the money. Soon after, he left for the West, afraid the Russians would come back. He could not take the risk of being arrested by them. They would surely send him away, maybe to a prisoner camp, because of his important military rank.

Emil took the cabinet home and researched the provenance. There was little information in his books, so he went back to the castle to visit the countess, who remained there. Emil could tell she had been a beautiful woman in her youth in the way she moved with grace and discipline from room to room. She sat composed in her red velvet tufted chair, poured a cup of tea for Emil, and told him the story of her family's acquisition of the beautiful Chinese-style cabinet.

The cabinet was made by the order of Augustus the Strong in the seventeen hundreds. His fascination with Chinese style was influenced by the Chinese exports from the East to Europe. He commissioned many pieces of furniture and porcelain during his reign. The cabinet was a gift to the bishop of Fulda, who was related to her husband, the baron. It remained in their family until the baron sold it to the antique dealer.

Emil considered this to be one of his most important pieces in his collection. The Chinese motifs were whimsical scenes of Chinese daily life. The scenes were hand painted in bold colors on black lacquer. It stood several feet high and commanded attention.

Another interesting find had brought him to the house of a dear old friend, an archaeologist. He had discovered ancient Roman relics from a site in the Lombardy region of Italy. This was the Gothic Roman stone baptismal bath.

His children, who had taken over the house when he passed on, invited Emil to a party. The house was cluttered with artifacts from their father. Emil looked outside at the garden and noticed the statues. Weeds covered the ground, and vines climbed so high and thick they wrapped around the statues. Emil had to pull the vines away from his face just to see them. The garden must have been beautiful when his friend was alive. Now his children did not care at all about the garden.

Emil noticed an object buried halfway into the ground. It was a dirty rectangular marble stone sculpture.

"I would like to buy the stone bath," Emil said. His friend's children simply shrugged their shoulders, surprised at any offer for the forgotten garden item.

"If you can dig it up and haul it away, it is yours to keep for free."

Emil was elated by their gesture. They had no idea of the value of the sculpture. They didn't care at all. Emil thought he would go back again and see what other treasures he could find. At least his dear friend would be pleased his treasure was going to somebody who appreciated it.

Chapter 23

Emil got used to being watched. He noticed the cars parked across the street each day. He did not care. He thought he was untouchable. This arrogant and carefree attitude caused him to be careless. Sometimes, he would forget to lock his front door and would dismiss it without concern. His friends cautioned him to be careful. Sometimes, he listened to them and stayed home.

This particular evening, he did not enjoy being alone. The solitude made him nervous. He paced through each room, scrutinizing his paintings that hung on the wall. He stared at the painting of his son. He had painted him when he was two years old. He wore a sweater with stripes in the middle, blue shorts, beige knickers, and little booties. In one hand, he held a teddy bear and in the other an apple. He remembered Max was seated on the floor. His blond hair was trimmed neatly around his ears. He captured on canvas Max's big brown eyes focused with curiosity as he sat quietly during the entire time he was painting him. Emil wept in the silence.

Emil missed his family. He was getting older. It was 1972. Emil was sixty-two years old, and Max was twenty-four. He missed all the years when Max was growing up and becoming a man, studying at the university, and getting married. Now Max was living in the United States.

He had let this happen—all by himself. He was a failure as a father. He had always put himself first. He did not think about the repercussions it would have on their relationship in the years to come. Somehow, he had to make it right. But for now, he was stuck behind the wall.

Chapter 24

Emil smiled at the Madonna he had placed tenderly on top of a wall stand across his bed. He lingered as if to say a prayer to her. He walked over to the table and started to shift various objects from one place to another. He was methodical in his approach and did not stop until each object was in perfect position.

He drank his coffee at the table while admiring the vase of white Oriental chrysanthemums in front of him. He searched for his reading glasses, only to find them on top of his head, and he scribbled on his notepad what he had planned to do today.

Then he moved to the kitchen to have breakfast with his mother. She had aged too. Her hands trembled a little, and her body ached when she stood for a long time, but she was still alert and loved to talk about her daily activities. They shared cheese and ham with crusty bread and sweet butter.

After breakfast, Emil took his daily walk to the store to pick up the morning newspaper. It reported only local and GDR news since the press was controlled by the state. All the communications were state run and based in East Berlin, even though reception of Western radio and television broadcasts were widespread.

He stopped at his favorite café and drank coffee with friends. They sparred over life's follies, except politics. You never knew who was listening to the conversations. Life was becoming mundane—a horrible situation he never thought he would allow himself to fall into.

Emil did not like feeling so moody. That afternoon, he decided to visit Arnstadt, south of Erfurt. An elderly aristocrat, Mr. Haus, wanted him to come to his estate to buy some tapestries. He hoped Emil would pay well for them.

Gustav drove a short distance on the autobahn then exited onto a small road that took him three kilometers onto a dirt road that led to a gigantic gray-stone house with a red-tile roof. Emil was delighted to see the beautiful Gothic architecture. It was six windows wide and four levels high. The entrance was in the front building on the ground floor. The next levels had balconies on each of the three sides. The balconies were covered with an arched roof, and french doors opened onto each balcony. The top balcony had spires at the top on each side. The top-floor windows were rectangular in shape. A triangular-shape window formed a peak at the top.

He stood transfixed by the macabre beauty. His mind drifted to the Gothic civilization, between the twelfth and sixteenth centuries. Starting from Northern France, the Goths had spread through Western Europe. Emil lifted the heavy round iron open handles and knocked on the huge door.

A distinguished gentleman opened the door. "Please, Mr. Diesel, come into my humble home."

"Thank you, Mr. Haus."

Together, they walked past an entire wall filled with portraits of family members and into a large foyer with a winding staircase. He observed that each side opened into another larger room. Those rooms opened up into even larger rooms. He could not see the end of the house. To the right and left of each room were archways that opened into other smaller rooms. Emil gasped when he saw the tapestries hanging from the walls. Some were large, four meters by three meters, and others were smaller, two-by-four meters.

One small tapestry caught his attention. Three borders alternated in a graduated width of red, blue, and gold. The scene pictured a young man and woman seated on a stone pedestal chair. The gentleman's blue cloak fell loosely around his shoulders and body. The woman wore a small cape at her shoulders draped over a loose long dress that covered her ankles, and she wore sandals on her feet. The background was filled with fruit trees and exotic plants with fanned leaves. They appeared to be holding a smaller tapestry of their daughter, who was surrounded by a different scene. A begging dog was at her side, mountains to her left, and a tree of large yellow flowers to her right—*a scene within a scene.*

Emil sighed, overcome with sadness. He thought of his own son living so far away, the same as the daughter in the tapestry. The weave was fine in detail and the colors vivid and bold. He gave the gentleman a very good price for such an incredible tapestry. He was elated.

Gustav saw a different man enter the car. Emil was smiling. He couldn't wait to hang the tapestry in his home and make it part of the family.

Marlene hurried upstairs; she did not want to be late for dinner with Emil and his mother. During dinner, she talked about her studies in restoration and complimented Emil on his most interesting new acquisition. After his mother retired to bed, Marlene joined Emil in the living room.

"Emil, I'm all yours now," she said, sensing his need for her.

"I missed you, Marlene."

Sitting by the fireplace, they sipped on rum from the antique glasses with the initial *M* on them—the ones he got in Weimar. Marlene gave Emil all her attention and no other when she was with him.

"Tell me a story, Emil."

"I love you, Marlene." Touched by her attention, he told her the story about the tapestry he acquired.

"I love you too, Emil." She took such delight in the stories Emil shared with her, and he was delighted to answer her questions. She loved Emil because he was always there waiting for her—so different from her other lovers, who walked in and out of her life.

They went to bed and curled up in each other's arms—so tight they could feel each other's hearts beating. He was gentle as he caressed her breasts, and as his hands followed the curves of her body, it ached with desire, and her lips quivered as she moaned. He gave her such pleasure.

Marlene turned around and lay on top of him. She kissed him with a desperate passion. Her longing could not be denied. As she thrust back and forth with such force, he cried out in ecstasy. They slept without waking until morning.

"Good morning, my sweet Marlene. All is well with life."

She smiled back, arms entwined around his neck. "Yes, all is well."

Chapter 25

Marlene was thirty years old and still lived downstairs. When she was a young woman in her twenties, Emil sent her to school in Dresden to study ballet. She was a wonderful dancer and performed in plays. She left ballet school because she had begun to gain weight; they had to let her go. She did not care; it was not what she wanted to do anyway. In the sixties, Emil insisted she go to art school. She chose to study art restoration because there was more opportunity for work in that field. She studied hard and became a very good restorer. She worked in Erfurt, restoring church altars.

Her friendly West German affiliates offered to fund her work restoring the churches since the East Germans were not interested in funding church restoration projects. They had no use for the church. They remained neutral with restraint.

Emil was Marlene's first love. She could never leave him. Her loyalty remained firm, even though she did have her German boyfriends and her Russian boyfriends. She made sure they were never local. She traveled to different parts of East Germany overnight so that none of her boyfriends bumped into each other.

Marlene had a boyfriend in Berlin. Hans was tall and handsome, like a movie star. He was a restorer and worked with her in Berlin, restoring a church altar in a Catholic church. He traveled to London, France, and other countries in Europe, giving speeches about his art restoration. At first she was suspicious of his travels until she realized he was never stopped at the border. She found out he was a Stasi informer for East Germany. She spent many nights with him in Berlin.

Marlene was a secretive, smart, and witty girl. Her beauty was captivating. Her boyfriends indulged her every whim. Marlene took full advantage of their offers, and they took full advantage of her. She had to keep herself healthy, happy, and safe. *Safety* was the key operative word for herself and for her dear Emil.

Survival was everyone's first priority under the East German regime. No one really knew if Marlene was picked up and asked to be an informer. She confided in no one. She was suspect, which could explain her frequent visits to Berlin and her new boyfriend in Berlin. She was smart indeed. If Hans did recruit her to be an informer, she remained under the radar. No one close to her knew about her relationships with her German and Russian boyfriends, and she always remained loyal to Emil.

The mysterious Marlene appeared unaffected by the restrictions of the regime. If the Stasi was watching her or waiting for her, they had a whole new network in play.

Chapter 26

The Stasi watched Emil from a distance. He felt safe and lived well, considering the conflicting times of the Honecker era—stability through control. If you were loyal to the Communist Party, you got a good job. If you were not loyal, you were excluded from that privilege.

The economy was wavering. The East German mark was weakening in the international market. The regime needed hard currency to buy goods from abroad. The people were getting nervous as they realized their money was losing value while those in the West were prospering. The regime was moving into desperate times.

The GDR had to find ways to acquire hard currency from the West. In 1973, they began confiscating the property of private collectors. The collectors were accused of violating GDR tax laws. When they couldn't pay the additional tax bill, usually a million or more East German marks, their artwork was confiscated and taken to the state-owned gallery—Old World Antiques and Art. It was a gallery filled with precious *stolen* art to be bought and sold.

The GDR's most prolific procurer of hard currency, Wilhelm Hahnentor, would sell the looted artwork to wealthy clients in the West, guaranteeing foreign currency for the Communist Party, SED.

The East Germans managed the sale of artwork under *strict secrecy*. Yet among the elite art circles of the West, word spread that artwork on the other side of the Wall was for sale.

Wilhelm Hahnentor took small groups of interested parties from the West to the small town of Bernauer, where huge warehouses were built for the state gallery. It was close to West Berlin. Truckloads of looted artwork—baroque furniture, porcelain, jewelry, coins, paintings, and rugs—taken from East German collectors were stored there to be sold to the highest bidder.

It was an incredible treasure hunt for the Western visitors.

Emil continued to buy art. His collection was flourishing until that fateful day on November 8, 1973, when his life changed forever.

Alfred stopped his car outside Emil's house. The sun had disappeared into the horizon. He sat motionless, leaving the engine to idle for several minutes. He muttered, "What can I do? I have no choice." He turned the engine off. He felt his stomach tighten and twist. Nausea overcame him. He lowered his hand and wrapped his fingers again around the key. He turned the key all the way; the engine started.

Thoughts filled his mind. *If I leave now, they will never know I was here. I cannot go through with this! Emil is a good man. How can I do this to him? It's not right.*

He started to pull away from the curb. Across the street, someone in a gray sedan flicked its lights on and off. His body shuddered as his jaw clenched. He felt his teeth grind together. Hands trembling, he pulled his car back onto the side of the curb.

They've followed me. They must have several cars watching me. He did not recognize the gray sedan.

I thought I was outsmarting them, but they've outsmarted me. The muscles in his body ached from the tension he felt. He squeezed his head with his hands. *My head aches!* He was about to lie to a man who had done nothing wrong.

Alfred had conducted business with Emil before. He liked Emil because he was fair, generous, and a man of his word.

I have no choice. They will hurt me if I do not follow their instructions.

The Stasi had their own set of rules—rules set in motion through manipulation.

Alfred got out of his car, buttoned his worn-out old coat, and pulled it tight around him. It was cold, and the chill went right through him. He walked to the back of his car and opened the trunk. He lifted a wooden figure, wrapped in sheets of plastic and covered with a coarse blanket, out of the trunk. He placed it on the ground and closed the hood with both hands. He stared at the figure. His body froze. He did not want to take another step. He turned around, hesitated, and walked toward the stairs, climbing one foot at a time up to the door with the figure secure in his hands. He knocked on the door once and then twice again.

Emil opened the door wide and encouraged him to come in from the cold. "Alfred, how wonderful it is to see you. Let me take this from you."

Alfred handed him the piece. He stuttered, "Thank you." *Why does he have to be so pleasant?*

Emil placed the figure on the side of a table in the living room. Alfred cowered as Emil placed his arms around him, hugging him. He did not realize how much he needed that hug.

His body relaxed, and his breathing finally slowed down. *If I am going to have Emil believe me, I must stay focused on what I have to do.*

"Emil, I need to sell this sculpture *today*. It is in fine condition, and I will take any price."

Emil sensed his old friend was desperate. "It is very interesting. Where did you get it?"

"I acquired it from a dealer in Arnstadt a long time ago." Alfred was in agony because he had just lied to him. Emil wanted him to stay and have a drink with him.

"I can't, Emil."

"Oh, come on. One vodka."

Alfred agreed because a drink sounded like a good idea at that moment. Inside, his body was shaking.

Emil scrutinized the piece. It was a fine sculpture of a saint. He admired the colors in the draped robe around its body. "They have not faded too much, and there are only a few cracks around the head by the ears. This saint has a handsome face too." Emil bought the sculpture and was more than happy to help a friend in need.

Alfred sighed. "This is wonderful. My family will be pleased."

"These are tough times," Emil said. "I feel fortunate to be working and making a steady pay. Collecting art helps me to keep my dream alive. Here is your money."

Alfred insisted it was not necessary to write a receipt for the statue. Emil thought it was unusual, but he did not think anything of it. Alfred must have had his reasons.

Emil had no idea of the trouble that was about to come his way. Alfred knew, and he realized he had just betrayed a friend. What could he do? Once he was out the door, his head dropped toward his chest in shame. The guilt was unbearable.

He saw the gray sedan pull away from the opposite side of the street. He ran to the driver's door, opened it, and jumped into the car as if his life depended on it. He shut his eyes tight. Tears stung as he wept. Taking a deep breath, he turned the key, flipped the lights on, and pulled away from the curb into the street. He hit the gas pedal and took off.

Three days passed. Emil woke up early, had his coffee at his table, and looked over some notes he had written about the saint. He would do more research in the afternoon after he met with his friends at the café. The saint was old, and he was eager to investigate its provenance.

He had breakfast with his mother as usual. She told him Gustav was driving her to the doctor's to pick up some medicine for her cough. She hoped she would be back before he returned home.

When he walked to his bedroom to dress, he passed through the dining room and living room. He enjoyed looking at each piece of his art that he had collected through the years. He stopped and picked up a red-chalk drawing that leaned against the wall, studying it and putting it back where it had lain. He reached for a small German porcelain figure of a young woman. He gently stroked the smooth ruffles and the delicate hand-painted flowers that adorned the dress and cape around her shoulders. He stepped carefully over the marble Roman figure lying on the floor and knelt beside it, imagining it lying underneath the earth for centuries until it was found.

Only art could be so well-preserved, he thought. This was his passion. Art gave him so much pleasure. He was a very happy man.

Emil gathered his coat and was ready to take his walk. He reached for a pen and placed it in his pocket. He loved to doodle on the napkins and newspapers at the café.

He heard several knocks on the door. He looked at the clock. It was ten o'clock. He opened the door. There stood two tall police officers in a firm, erect pose. They were in their black starched uniforms and matching hats. Their arms pushed open the door with such force that it knocked him to one side.

"Officers, what can I do for you?"

They stared Emil down. He was not afraid yet. They walked into the living room. Their boots, wet from the rain, soaked the rugs. Their mouths opened wide as their eyes surveyed the room. They saw art everywhere, from floor to ceiling.

One police officer spoke, "Are you Emil Diesel?"

"Yes, I am." He was bewildered by their formality and confused by the abruptness of their entrance and speech.

The taller police officer gestured with his hands.

"We found out through our sources that you acquired a sculpture of a church figure this month. This figure was stolen from a church in Turin."

"I bought it from a client."

"Mr. Diesel, it is a crime to secure stolen goods. You have in your possession stolen art from a church."

"I did not know it was stolen. My client bought it from a dealer a while ago, kept it in his home, and wanted to sell it. He needed money, and I wanted to help him. That is all. I am a collector. I buy antiques from stores and auctions, and sometimes I buy from people who have art they want to sell."

Emil knew he did not have a bill of sale for the sculpture; this was his mistake. He would not give them the name of his client because Alfred would get into trouble.

The police officer pulled out a small book from his pocket. They did not believe him. The officer asked for his client's name. He had to give it up. It was the only way to clear up this misunderstanding. Emil gave them his client's name—Alfred Flicker.

"He will clear this all up. He will tell you that he sold the object to me."

"We will locate him and find out if you are telling us the truth," the police officer said. "In the meantime, Mr. Diesel, you need to come to the police station until we can reach him." The police escorted him out of the room. There was no one to call. Everyone was gone. He was sure he could call home later from the station.

He could not believe what was happening to him. They walked him to the car, and with one hand on his shoulder and one on his head, they shoved him into the back seat. The other police officer went back into the house and took the statue.

"This is evidence," he said, responding to Emil's reaction.

No one spoke. There was dead silence all around him.

Why is this happening to me? I do not understand.

The two-kilometer ride to police headquarters seemed like the longest ride of Emil's life.

The two police officers escorted him into headquarters. They sat him down at the desk in the far corner of the room. They gave their paperwork to the officer at the desk and walked away.

The officer continued to interrogate Emil. "Mr. Diesel, tell me how you came to have a stolen church figure in your home."

Emil told the same story again. "Alfred Flicker brought it to my house. He was eager to sell the sculpture because he needed money." He told them over and over that he bought the figure from Alfred.

"Mr. Diesel," the officer said, "you told Alfred to steal the statue and bring it to your house."

Emil stood up. "That is not true."

The officer ignored him.

Emil Diesel was not allowed to make a phone call or send a message to his lawyer and family. Nobody came to his defense. He was ordered to go to a detainment center to a jail until further investigation. He stayed behind iron bars for six months.

Chapter 27

Emil squinted as he tried to focus. He surveyed the small empty room. Fright took over his senses. All he could see was four cement walls and a small window with bars. His body trembled when he realized this jail was a living hell. He was imprisoned in the obscure darkness, and the guards peered through a small opening in the cell door to see him. That night, they played loud, desolate music and strange chilling sounds from the loudspeaker outside his cell. He couldn't sleep. The sounds seemed to penetrate through his mattress. Emil scanned his room again, his eyes still trying to adjust to the darkness. In one corner of the cold rectangular cell was the pail for his excrement. Diagonally across from the pail was his small cot. His eyelids felt so heavy. He was so tired. There was no more fight in him. Sleep took over.

When he opened his eyes, he could not remember what day it was. He thought, *Is it the next day or the day after that?* He was all mixed up. The guard passed a kind of clumpy porridge, a piece of hard white bread, and water to him through the small opening in the door. He forced himself to eat then lay down across his bed to sleep.

Time seemed to pass him by. The guards walked by often to wake him up. Soon he was walking back and forth in his cell to keep his blood circulation moving in his legs. He sat on the floor and stretched his body out just to keep it from stiffening. At night, the dampness and cold were unbearable, causing his body to shiver. The cell stunk of waste, and he would ask the guards to take it away as often as they could. Emil tried to keep his mind quiet despite the noise. He thought about his art, picturing every detail of each piece in his mind as he walked through his house.

"This is worse than what I had endured during the war," he said out loud. No one was listening to him. He was alone. He had no idea what was happening on the outside, nor could he understand why no one had come to help him get out.

I do not want to die here.

His mother was frantic when Emil did not come home. It was getting late, and it was not like him to miss dinner. Marlene came through the door, quite upset. She was sobbing as she blurted out the news.

"Frieda, Emil is in jail. A friend of mine found out from one of the officers at police headquarters that Emil was taken to the station for questioning. He was interrogated. They arrested him and sent him to jail. He is detained there pending further investigation."

Shocked, Frieda broke down and cried.

"I was told a church pastor from Turin called the police and told them a statue was taken from the altar of their church. A week had gone by before they noticed it was missing. The police received information about the person who had the stolen statue. They came to your house, took Emil into custody for the theft, and confiscated the statue. Emil denied he stole the statue, but they did not believe him. Emil pleaded with them to find Mr. Flicker, the one who sold him the statue. They are detaining him until they find Flicker and learn the truth." Marlene had finished talking, but her body still trembled all over.

Frieda was confused. Nothing made sense. "My son would never take art that did not belong to him. Marlene, you must help Emil."

"I will try. I believe Emil. His client must have stolen the statue from the church. I will call Emil's lawyer, Dr. Karl Gunter. He will know what to do. Don't worry. Try to get some sleep, Frieda."

That evening, Marlene called Emil's friends and told them what had happened to Emil. No one could believe it.

"We warned him to be careful, Marlene. The Stasi were watching him." His friends cared about him and wanted to know what they could do to help.

"I don't know. I don't know. I'll keep in touch," she said.

Marlene had a sleepless night. For weeks, she had heard rumors in the network that something was going to happen concerning an art dealer. She never thought it was Emil, who was a collector. She thought she had protected him and had kept him away from the Stasi. She was wrong. She had to help Emil get out of jail, and she had to be careful how she did it. Marlene had two loyalties—one to Emil and one to herself. One was unconditional and one conditional.

She called Dr. Gunter, his lawyer, who was also a dear friend of Emil's. She also called the director and curators of the Gera Museum to help Emil. Dr. Gunter went to local police headquarters to hear their version of the story. He wanted to know why they had detained Emil in jail.

The officer on duty informed Dr. Gunter they had found the evidence in his house and were looking for Mr. Flicker, who allegedly sold the statue to Emil. Emil would remain in jail while they investigated. He gave Dr. Gunter a copy of the report and Emil's statements. The officer told him they would keep him informed of their investigation. That never happened. The local police answered to the Stasi.

The director and curators gave their statements to the police regarding Emil's character. They praised him for his integrity, his artistic and moral values, his kindness to others, and more. His friends did the same. It did not do any good. Emil remained in jail.

Dr. Gunter was not allowed to see Emil, and his only witness, Alfred Flicker, still had not been found. The police made it very difficult for him to argue his case in his defense. He surmised the Stasi wanted something; the police investigation was taking too long. It was not that difficult to find someone in East Germany. He had a gut feeling Emil was set up. But why? He had to find Flicker. They kept feeding him false reports as to the whereabouts of Flicker. The police were stalling. They did not want him to investigate on his own.

Chapter 28

Emil lost track of time. The isolation was killing him. He was not used to being by himself. He thought back through the years when he had stayed by himself for any duration. He could not recall a time when he was alone like this. He always had friends and family around him. Nannies were always around when Max and Marie were small, and Gustav was with him so long that he, too, had become part of the family.

I miss my mother, he thought with such sadness. *She must be so upset. I hope Marlene moved upstairs to keep her company. I hope she talks to her at breakfast as I did. I hope she takes good care of her while I sit here in this godforsaken cell.*

Emil fought back the tears as they fell down his face. His arm brushed them away, angry at his stupidity. His elbows supported his head, and he bellowed and cursed for letting this incident happen.

I should have insisted on a bill of sale from Alfred.

His memory drifted to Amsterdam. He was never alone there either. He was young, enthusiastic, and filled with life. Art filled up every space of his loneliness.

"It was a glorious place. Now look at me," he talked out loud. Emil threw his water cup across the room in disgust. "How many more days must I be here?" he shouted to no one.

The cold ran through him, and his joints stiffened. He ached all over. He rose from his bed and stretched his painful body. He paced back and forth many times from one end of the cell to the other until he felt the warmth again.

The guard rapped at his door and passed him food and water through the small opening.

"Wait, please. Tell me what day this is?" Emil said.

"It is better you do not know," the guard answered back. "It will just make it more difficult for you to stay here. Trust me, it is for your own good." Emil was surprised to see him showing a little compassion.

He lay down and closed his eyes. He wanted to dream that he was not in his cell. He wanted to dream he was home, sitting by the fire and sipping his rum. He could almost feel the heat of the fire against his body and the taste of the rum on his tongue. He pictured the husband and wife sitting at a table in his seventeenth-century Dutch painting by David Teniers. He was holding a glass of white wine in his hand, and his wife was pointing to something written on a piece of parchment. The scene reminded him of home and Marlene.

Any light that passed through the barred window was gone. It was dark and cold. He wrapped his arms around his shivering body beneath his thin cover. He tried to sleep before the loud, haunting music of death filled his cell and his head. His mind drifted. His eyes closed. Fatigue and loneliness surrounded him like a warm blanket.

Chapter 29

While Emil sat in jail, something was about to happen at his house.

It was a beautiful sunny day compared to the usual dreary and cold days of winter. Without their hats and scarves, neighbors took their walks, chatting about their families as they enjoyed the rays of the sun wrap around their bodies. They passed by houses with open windows to let the fresh air in. Curtains fluttered as the breeze flowed through the rooms.

Frieda was in the kitchen, preparing lunch for Gustav and the house cleaner. There was not a day, an hour, or a minute when she did not think about Emil. Marlene had told her Emil had been set up, but she could not understand why Emil was still in jail.

From the window, Frieda heard quite a commotion going on outside. She stretched her old, somewhat limber body halfway out the window and saw two black sedans and two vans pull into the curb by the sidewalk. Marlene noticed too and rushed upstairs.

Several men in plainclothes left their cars and walked toward the impressive red door. They looked up at the stately house. One man, stiff and poised, climbed the wide steps to finish what they had set out to do.

Loud knocks echoed from the door. Marlene felt her hands shaking as she ran down to open the door. The assertive man motioned with his hand for the other men to join him.

His tone was official. "We have the authority to enter your house to take an inventory of Emil Diesel's art collection," he said. "We have reason to believe Mr. Diesel operated as an art dealer without reporting it to the proper authorities. This action is considered an illegal act under the regime."

"This is absurd. Emil works for the government as a graphic illustrator. He is a collector of art, not a dealer." Marlene remained cool. She knew he was a Stasi officer. "He would not be so foolish as to compromise his job and integrity just to cheat the East German government."

"That may be the case," the Stasi officer said. "Until we hear otherwise, we are authorized by the finance department to take an inventory of his art collection."

"May I see your papers?"

He showed her papers justifying entry into Emil's home. It all appeared legal, but Marlene knew they could justify any search with or without papers.

Four solicitors from the state; a curator; the director, Dr. Hans Brewer, from the Gera Museum; one man from the finance department; and one woman, Frau Meyer, from the government state-owned art gallery Old World Antiques and Art followed the Stasi officers into the house.

Their eyes were fixed upon the bounty of art before them. The director was shocked by Emil's accumulation of art since his return to Erfurt. The curator whispered to the director his extreme pleasure as they walked through each room. Every one of them was astonished by the diversity of his collection from all over the world, each piece more important than the one before. There had to be thousands of pieces of art—statues and paintings, rare books and drawings, coins, silver cups and bowls, porcelain figures, and Chinese vases.

They had not seen a vast collection like this anywhere outside of a museum. It was clear to the director that the finance agent looked at the collection and saw tax money. The solicitors looked at the collection and saw hard Western currency. It was not good for their museum.

Marlene watched them and heard it all. She shook her head, repulsed by the trap they had set. Now she understood why Emil was targeted as an art dealer and detained in jail. The regime was desperate for hard currency. They wanted to seize Emil's collection and sell all of it.

The curator and director were salivating at the thought of the art they could put into the Gera Museum. They tagged items for themselves as they moved through the art. Emil was in jail. They could take their time and conduct a thorough inventory.

They completed their tour through the house. No one had to say anything. The director and curator were all smiles, and the sinister looks of the finance and art gallery agents said it all. The Stasi informed Marlene they would be back again in a few days to start the inventory.

On Monday morning, the Stasi arrived at the door with extra security guards armed with guns. The curators came in vans from the Gera Museum. The word had spread fast in East Germany. They came from Berlin and Dresden too. They specialized in different areas of art and antiquities from around the world, past and present.

Each one carried a notebook in their hands. They catalogued each item by number and description, such as porcelain or sculpture, and a date of acquisition was attached. A current appraisal was entered last by the curators.

The curators were drooling and arguing over which items of art they wanted to take for their museum. Frau Meyer from the state-owned gallery was calculating how much art she would sell to the West for hard currency. The finance agent was adding up the value of the art and the tax money it would bring in for the regime.

They all wanted a piece. The curators and agents became jealous and greedy. The government agencies and the museums fought daily over almost two thousand individual pieces of Emil's collection.

It took months for them to complete the inventory.

Each day, Frieda and Marlene could do nothing but watch them as they took over the house. They came midmorning and left by 1500 hours (three o'clock). On one occasion, Frieda heard shouting coming from the living room.

One of the curators from the Dresden museum was arguing with the woman from the government agency.

"You cannot take the bath sculpture. It is too valuable. It belongs in my museum." His finger was pointing at her face. "Roman sculptures are hard to get here, and they need its proper place in a museum. You cannot sell it to the West. I do not care how much currency you can get for it."

The agent stomped her feet and said, "I don't care. If we want to take it, we will take it. We will see who has more say in this matter."

The security guard walked over to them. "Stop arguing and get back to work. I do not want to be here all day."

At the end of Emil's fifth month in jail, the small army of government agents, security guards, and museum staff had completed their job. The curators looked distraught because for them, it had become a labor of love. They understood Emil's passion as a collector. A few of the curators, especially the Gera Museum director, who now sported a fine goatee, felt sorry for him. He could only imagine how it must feel to lose such a collection.

Forty years of work was lost. All agreed it was a travesty.

"Too bad," they said with sad, pitiful-looking faces.

At the same time, they were thinking only of themselves and of what they would gain in prestige and power when Emil's art was placed in their museums. As for the agents from the state-owned gallery and the finance department, it was all about the money.

Chapter 30

It was the beginning of May 1974. Six months in jail had been difficult for Emil. Most of the time, he lay down in utter despair on his cot. His nutrition was poor, and he had lost a considerable amount of weight. His uniform hung off his frail body. He moved around his cell at a slow pace now, his energy reduced to a fraction of what it was.

Often he became confused and irrational, pounding his head against the frame of his cot because of the loud music ringing in his ears all night. In the darkness, in his lucid moments, he also had time to think about what he had become—a failure, a disappointment. He could feel his self-confidence, even his zest for life, becoming depleted. Yet his love of art never wavered. He built his collection despite the horrendous times, and *he still could dream*.

Emil thought about his mother, Marlene, and the direction his life took after his many indiscretions. He missed Zelda and hoped her life was happy in Düsseldorf.

He thought about Maximilian. *I was not a good father. I was too harsh with him, too impatient, too quick with my hand.* "When I get out, I will be a better one," he shouted out loud, his words evaporating into the stale air around him. *This is a promise to Max and to myself. I will make things right between us, if it's not too late.*

Emil realized he had to let go of his obsession to possess art. He had allowed this preoccupation—this mania—to control his life. Look where it got him—in jail. Now he felt old and tired. As a young man, he always lived his life fast and vibrant. His views of life had become distorted the more his collection grew. This obsession was not good for him anymore.

Security and happiness were in place all along for me to enjoy. I could not notice what was right in front of me. He was foolish. Love, family, and good friends were always around him to feed his body, mind, and soul. His art was never meant to replace them.

It was the last day of May. The odd guard approached his cell door. He unlocked it and entered the cell. Emil stood up from his bed. He walked slowly, his feet shuffling toward the guard.

The guard reached out, gripped his hand, and shook it. "Mr. Diesel, you are free to go."

Bewildered, Emil held his head high as he walked out of his cell. It was difficult to keep pace alongside of the guard. He felt an uncontrollable grin cover his face. He was free to go home at last.

The guard led him to a secure office. He sat down across from the Stasi officer who handed him his signed release papers.

"Emil Diesel, you are released from detainment. After a thorough investigation, we found your witness, Alfred Flicker. Your client confessed to the theft of the statue from the church. You understand? He confessed." He watched Emil's face.

Stunned, Emil showed no expression.

"He said you had no idea that the art was stolen when you acquired it from him. He said he was desperate for money. We apologize for detaining you these past months. The investigation took longer than we thought. I am authorized by the East German government to compensate you for your lost wages and time spent in detention. You are free to go home."

Emil was not only confused he was angry. They detained him for six cruel months, and all he got was an apology and compensation? It was ridiculous! There had to be more to the story than what they were telling him. He needed to get home right away.

"I'm ready to go." Defiant, he stormed out of the office.

The guard rushed to his side to steady him and lead him to the door. Emil pushed the door open with the strength he had left.

Nervous, Marlene stood there at the entrance, waiting to take him home. When she saw Emil, she could not stop the tears of sheer joy from flowing over her cheeks. She wrapped her arms around him and cried. He cried uncontrollably. He was so relieved to leave this part of his life behind him for good. An anxious Gustav waved to them to come to the car so he could take them home.

Gustav helped Emil into the car. Holding back his tears, he blurted out, "It is so good to see you again. We need you home. It has not been the same without you."

He noticed Emil looked thin and weary; his face was pale and drawn. He came out an old man. He was only sixty-two.

The ride home was quiet. Emil could feel the warmth from the sun fill the car and take over his chilled body. He closed his eyes and breathed in the fresh air of spring, letting the air flow slowly out from his mouth. He took several deep breaths. He opened his eyes slowly, squinting from the bright sun as it peeped through the white billowy clouds.

He looked around and saw nothing had changed, just the weather. People dressed in thin colorful shirts were out walking their dogs and enjoying the day. He thought life had gone on as usual while he was in jail.

As they approached the house, Emil saw that some things had changed. The small lawn to the left of the stairs was full of weeds, and parts were cut up with dirt exposed. The stairs needed washing, and the windows were cloudy and dirty.

Finally, they were home. Gustav pulled the car alongside the curb. Marlene raced to his side to help him. Carefully, she opened the door. Emil turned his body sideways and slowly lifted himself out. With Gustav's help, he staggered up the stairs, feeling every painful step under his feet. He was eager to get inside.

At the door, his mother waited with open arms. They both cried when they saw each other. He was exhausted. The reunion was all too much for him. He went into the kitchen, seeking his chair to sit by the table.

Frieda served Emil a good plate of dark crusty bread, headcheese, salami, and ham. A large cold beer accompanied the meal. He was hungry, but he took only one small bite at a time, determined to eat everything on his plate. He washed the food down with the dark beer. He placed his hands on his tummy, letting out a sigh of satisfaction.

He still was disoriented. His memory was vague, and his thoughts were scattered in what seemed like a maze of cobwebs. His eyes wandered around his home. At last, relief overcame him. He stumbled his way to his room. Marlene rushed to help him.

"I need to sleep now. I am tired. We will have plenty of time to talk later."

Hours passed. Frieda glanced at the clock. She was eager to wake him.

"Let him wake up on his own," Marlene said. "He will be himself when he wakes up and sees his art. *He will be happy again.*"

"We must tell him what happened here. He has to know," Frieda said.

Emil slept all afternoon and night. When he woke up the next day, it was almost noon. He was not sure if he had slept without waking. Still groggy from many hours of sleep, he reached for the glass of water on his bedside table and drank it all without stopping. He gathered his thoughts while his eyes wandered around his room. All his cherished art surrounded him.

He was overwhelmed. Yesterday, he was in a stark, empty cell pacing back and forth and counting steps. Today he was in his room, just as he left it, a free man.

This was a bad dream, he thought. His body trembled. *I fought demons, and the truth saved me.*

His stomach growled. He was famished. He shuffled his feet down the hallway as the smell of coffee drew him to the kitchen table. His mother was humming a children's tune as she poured him a cup of coffee. She set down in front of him a plate of eggs and bacon with dark bread. After he filled his stomach, he wanted his bed.

It seemed the stiffness and soreness had left his tired body. There was no loud, blaring music and no ringing in his ears. Lying in his bed, he fell into a deep, blissful sleep.

He woke up with a multitude of questions rattling in his head. He waited for Marlene to return home from work. He wanted to know what had happened at home while he was detained. He had trouble remembering details about the day when the police came and took him away.

He rested in his room for the remainder of the day. Seated at his desk, he tried to read notes that he had made to himself six months ago. But he was distracted by his recent memories—the anguish of isolation, the piercing sounds, the lack of humanity.

Home at last, Marlene ran upstairs to see Emil. They sat in their chairs by the fireplace, sipping vodka like it was a fine brandy and discussing the events that led to his detainment in jail. His mind was still hazy. Emil squeezed his eyes as he tried to force his thoughts out.

"I remember the police telling me they got a confession from Alfred. He stole the statue, not me. The Stasi accused me of being a dealer, but I do not understand what that had to do with the theft and my purchase of the statue."

"Your mother and I called your lawyer, Dr. Gunter, to take your case. He went to the police to find out why they detained you. He came back to the house, shaking his head. He said you were setup by the Stasi. Dr. Gunter investigated your case right away, but they kept stalling him. There was nothing he could do to get you out of jail." She stared into his eyes. "This is what happens when you go up against the Stasi and the regime."

She leaned closer to Emil. "The police must have seen all the art in the house when they took you away. Soon after, the Stasi came to look around. They accused you of operating as a dealer. Then they came back again. They began to take an extensive inventory of your collection. Don't you see? This is the real reason they went after you. They want your art for the regime."

He sipped his vodka, absorbing all this news. Emil was astonished by their shrewdness.

"I never saw it coming. I can't believe I was outwitted by them."

"Emil, they came back for months while you were in jail. They came during the week. The Stasi came with security guards with guns. Curators came from the museums, and agents from the state-owned gallery and finance department followed. They complied a notebook listing each piece of art you had collected since the twenties. They found your scribbled account books and used them to appraise each item. The entire ordeal sickened me," she said. "There was not a thing I could do. I am so sorry, Emil."

"Marlene, it is not your fault," he said.

"Emil, they finished the inventory only a few days ago. We got the call the next day that you were being released."

Emil rose from his chair and clenched his hands together. "I must be prepared for their next move. It's coming soon. They want my art. I have to stop them!" He began pacing back and forth then reached for the phone to call Karl.

Karl explained his case to Emil. "The regime has been targeting collectors and dealers to replenish their treasury. The taxes of a dealer are much higher than they are for a collector. They confiscate their art by hitting them with an enormous tax bill they know people cannot pay."

"I was cleared of all charges."

"They still claim you are a dealer even though you were cleared of all charges of theft of the statue. You do know that was just a setup."

Emil could not believe what he was hearing.

"I'm sorry," Gunter said. "Expect your bill soon."

Emil shoved the phone down so hard he almost broke it. His heart beat faster as he thought about the ramifications of the tax bill.

"If they had not done the inventory, I could have hidden my art. How clever of them to throw me in jail. There is nothing I can do now."

Marlene put her arm around him. "We will think of something."

"I need to lie down. My head is killing me." Back safe in his bed, Emil closed his eyes. It was quiet and peaceful in his room. A warm breeze passed over him as he fell into a deep sleep.

In his dream, he was running. He could not see because of the darkness. He kept tripping over objects on the road. He started kicking them aside. The objects were all different shapes and sizes, some soft and hard. He ran faster, this time falling on top of a motionless object. He felt his whole body stiffen. He pushed himself off, stumbling as he felt his way around to his feet. He felt a cold sweat at the back of his neck. He woke up frightened.

After dinner, Marlene returned upstairs to join Emil. She fell into the tufted armchair, crossing her legs underneath her. Emil handed her a glass of Russian vodka.

He was fuming. "I will not let them take my art away. I still have no plan." He tapped his fingers on the armchair. He always figured out a plan for any situation, but now he could not think. He hurled his glass onto the floor. It shattered.

"Stop, Emil!" Marlene left her chair. "This is driving you crazy."

Marlene went to get the broom. She swept up the broken glass. They sat together in silence. Color drained from his face. He helped himself to another drink.

"I'm sorry," he said. "Enough now. Let's talk about you."

Marlene trembled. Her mind was spinning. Should she tell him what she had done? No, his state of mind was too fragile. He might not understand. She would tell him later. She turned to him.

"I'm okay. My restoration work in Berlin is almost done. I love restoring the altar. No one bothers me. The hours are long, but it is rewarding work. While you were gone, I came as often as I could so your mother would not be alone. She is an amazing woman. She made meals for the men who were here without a comment. She took her walks and did not cry even though I knew she was afraid for herself and for you. Every day she asked if there was any news about you. Now you are home. She is singing again and wearing her pretty dresses."

Emil did not answer, but he smiled at her with appreciation. His head nodded off a few times before his eyes closed. Finally, he excused himself and went to bed alone.

Four days had passed since he returned home. As he wandered through each room, conversing with his art, he was certain that he had to reestablish a sense of normal life in his home for himself and for the ones he loved.

Chapter 31

His walk to the café seemed to take longer than usual. He was afraid to find out how much his friends knew about his absence. His beret tipped to one side of his head. He ambled down the cobblestone street, observing everything along the way.

The café was crowded. Cowering, he gestured to his friends who were having coffee by the window.

"Emil, join us." They waved him over. They watched Emil work his way around the tables toward them. Startled, they stood up, greeting him with huge hugs. "We were so worried about you. We heard about your arrest and knew it was a complete sham. You would never steal something you love. Come, friend. Sit down."

Their concern upset him so much that his hands trembled as he lowered himself into his chair like an old man. He did not like all the attention this time.

His mouth quivered. "It was an ordeal that I am trying hard to forget."

They continued to stare at him, eager to hear more. His hands shook. He couldn't look at them. He took a deep breath and told his story. They gasped in disbelief.

"You survived, dear friend. That's all that matters."

"I know. I take one day at a time."

They saw a broken man who sat motionless. An eerie feeling passed over them. Emil was not the same man.

He placed both hands on the arm of the chair and lifted himself up. He adjusted his beret and swung his arm to wrap his scarf around his neck. It wasn't there. He had forgotten it at home. It was so unlike him to forget his scarf. He collected his paper and waved back to them as he left the café. Sadness overcame him. He shuffled his worn-out feet all the way back to the house.

That afternoon, a young man wearing a white shirt, black pants, and red tie from the finance department came to his home, knocked on the door, and handed Emil a tax bill. He staggered back against the wall when he saw the amount. It was 1,200,000 Eastern marks. His hand went numb. The bill fell to the floor.

"They want 1,200,000 Eastern marks. This is absurd! I will fight. I only make two thousand marks a month. I cannot pay this bill, and I refuse to sell my art!" He grabbed his beret and scarf and rushed out the door, almost knocking the man down.

"Gustav, bring the car. We are going to my attorney."

Emil showed Karl his bill. He paced back and forth in front of his desk. "I want to fight this amount. I want you to write a letter to Erich Honecker. He is the general secretary in Berlin. Explain my case. Tell him I am not a dealer. I am a collector. Tell him I was set up."

Gunter hesitated, choosing his words carefully. "I'm sorry, Emil. It is a waste of time. It is not going to help," he said. "Look what they did to you."

Crazed, Emil said, "I am not going to let them beat me to the ground and step all over me. I must fight for my rights."

"Emil, you don't have any rights."

"Karl, I don't care. Send the letter, please."

Karl sent the letter to Berlin.

When the Stasi and the finance department found out about the letter, they intercepted it. To appease Emil, the head of the finance department contacted him and told him they would reduce the amount of the bill. They decreased Emil's bill by two hundred thousand marks.

"It's no use fighting us," he said.

Emil had no recourse but to pay one million marks for taxes they said he owed. There was no triumph, only defeat.

This was a crime. Emil had paid his taxes every year. There was never a problem until now. The GDR used their cunning tactics to force him to sell his art to pay his tax bill. More bad news shattered his spirit. He was not allowed to sell it to anyone but the state-run art gallery. He would never see his art again. Emil felt violated, stripped naked to the core of his existence.

Later at home, his mother tried to cheer him up. "Emil, my son, you can build your art collection again. Think of the challenge it will give you. You used to love a challenge."

Emil just sat there with a vacant expression on his face. She knew he did not hear one word of what she was saying. She put her arms around him and held him close. She was losing him to his own silent thoughts.

Marlene tried to cheer him up. She sat with him by the fireplace. She tried to distract him, asking him advice regarding her work or discussing with him a book she was reading. Nothing seemed to interest him. Her heart was breaking. Tears of hopelessness ran down her face. She felt so guilty these days. She had tried to protect him from what she knew about the setup, but her silence had imprisoned him instead.

Days passed into weeks. Emil remained in his house. His depression worsened. He stayed in bed longer after breakfast. He walked around in his pajamas and robe and spent the remainder of the day talking to his art. He did not want to talk to anyone. He ached all over. He was so tired that his bed and sleep became his only relief.

His eyes closed as if there were a heavy weight on them. One time, he remembered a dream. It was so vivid it startled him out of his sleep. He was in a storm of bullets. He tried to dodge them as they blew past him. He felt his body move one way then another. He heard yelling and screaming behind him. Death was not far behind. He moved quickly and stumbled over a body in the darkness. The rank smell of death filled his nostrils. A bolt of lightning passed through him to his very core. He felt every nerve shock his body.

He was jolted awake. It was strange to feel death. He quickly rose to his feet and walked to the open window. It was morning. The sky was deep blue, there were no clouds, and the air smelled sweet. He took a deep breath and looked down at his body. He was relieved to see no wound in his flesh.

He had survived death, or was this death?

Life is so precious, he thought, staring into the mirror. He had not shaved in days, and his pajamas reeked of sweat. Disgusted with himself, he shouted with conviction, "Feeling sorry for yourself is done. Look, I am still here. Have I survived jail only to create another one at home? *I can survive losing my art.* I have a mind and soul, and I have the courage to start over."

Emil showered and dressed in fresh pressed clothes. He ran his hand over his smooth-shaven face. He felt good for the first time in a long time. He sat down for breakfast and had an appetite for life again. He filled his plate and was satisfied. His mother turned to him with a smile on her face that she had not felt for a while.

Chapter 32

Marlene visited Emil after his epiphany. She saw a different man appear before her. His eyes had the sparkle she had grown to love through the years. He greeted her with a loving smile and hugged and kissed her passionately. She gasped for breath. His desire for her was so unexpected that she giggled and blushed like a young girl.

She returned his kiss with as much passion as his and with a hunger for love. She stepped back. "You look wonderful, Emil. I have been so worried about you."

"Something wonderful has happened. It has taken me some time to realize what was important and who was important in my life. Come sit down with me. Let's talk," he said.

They sat down by the fire. September nights were cooler now. The slow-burning fire took the chill out. He handed her a glass of champagne to celebrate what he called his second homecoming—his rebirth. Marlene thought it was the perfect time to tell him what she had done.

"I need to tell you a story. It is very important," Marlene said. "It is about your art."

Emil composed himself. "I am listening."

She sipped her champagne. "I had heard rumors in my circle of friends that a dealer of art was being investigated. I had no idea it was you. You are a collector, not a dealer." She could not look at him. "It happened so fast: the setup, the interrogation, the detainment in jail. I could do nothing to stop it. I felt so guilty because I did not tell you about the rumors before. After, I wanted to protect myself and you." Her teary eyes met his. "I was afraid. Later, I heard from my friends at the police station that the Stasi were coming to your house to look around. It was then I knew they were interested in your art. While your mother was gone one morning with Gustav, I went through the house and took various pieces of art. I tried to choose items of value and those you loved. I hid them in the storage facility behind the abandoned corner store. I took as much as I could out of the house without attracting suspicion."

Emil grinned. He was elated.

"Emil, I'm sorry I did not tell you right away, but you were not well when you came home."

"I wondered why I could not find some of my favorite pieces. I assumed the curators and others who were taking inventory took them for themselves. How can I be angry with you? Clearly, you saved them from their fate."

Marlene was relieved. "I can get them for you anytime."

"No, leave the art where it is. You must believe this place is safe where nobody can find it. When I have paid my tax bill, we will go together and get the collection."

They clinked their glasses satisfied that something good came out of a bad situation. Emil forgave her with another passionate kiss. She followed him to bed. She would be with him tonight and for as many nights as he wanted her.

Lying next to her, his thoughts drifted to his family who stood by him—his mother, Marlene, and Marie. He thought about Max.

He wondered if Max knew about his calamity. He would never tell him about his experience in jail, how bad it got for him. He hoped his son would never find out about this tragic episode in his life.

Chapter 33

During the next few months, Emil chose each piece with the highest value to bring to the state gallery. He wanted to get as much money as he could for them. He chose silver and gold items, icons that were adorned with gemstones mounted in silver, German figurines and furniture, and beautiful paintings by French, Italian, and Dutch artists. In the West, at auction, he knew they would bring in a good price. It was blood art for the West and blood money for the state. He chose his African art as well as his Greek and Roman antiquities. With a notebook in hand, Emil listed each item. Sometimes, he brought one item and, other times, items in lots. He was assigned to the state dealer Frau Meyer.

Five months had gone by. The days grew shorter, and the leaves fell. People on the street were bundling up their coats and wrapping scarves around their necks. It was hard to believe almost a year had gone by since that fateful day.

He was on a mission now. His outlook about life was better than months before. He was moving forward. His art was selling at top prices. He paid half his tax bill—about 500,000 marks.

There was so much corruption at the state level. Meyer, the state dealer, bought the artwork from Emil. Meyer paid the finance department who credited Emil's account. Then the artwork was sent to the secret warehouse in Bernauer, where it was sold to the West by the GDR, making enormous profits. The currency conversion from Western hard currency to Eastern German marks was ten to one. It seemed that no one knew or spoke of the Communists' plan to target private collectors.

The blood money all went to the regime to help stabilize the wavering economy in the GDR. At the same time, they did not want to jeopardize the West German foreign policy, which was begun in the late sixties, initiated by Willy Brandt. It was a policy of *détente* with the Soviet bloc countries, recognizing the East German government and expanding commercial relations with Soviet bloc countries. It was called *Ostpolitik* (Eastern Policy).

The museums were furious that they were not able to have any of the beautiful artwork. They made quite a scene over Emil Diesel's collection. They approached the state dealer and bullied her. It was useless. Meyer wanted it all. It was rumored the museums had found a way to keep some treasures for themselves.

Emil was filled with hope. He had amassed quite a large collection. He was confident he could pay his entire tax bill and still would have a considerable amount of art left. He thought about the objects that were hidden and felt like a rich man again.

Settling into his routine, he was convinced he would survive this terrible time in his life. He read through his art books and anticipated collecting again.

Emil selected with a discerning eye each piece of art that he brought to Meyer. He chose small statues of Roman figures and busts from ancient Greece. He surrendered his Chinese ceramic bowls and a bronze horse from the Ming Dynasty. He had a difficult time parting with the drawings by Picasso.

Gustav drove him to the agency with each piece. He was sympathetic toward Emil, no matter what the Stasi wanted him to do. He knew how much he loved his art.

Meyer was eager to see each museum-quality piece Emil brought to her. She secretly admired each piece; even she hated to part with it. She did meticulous research and documented each piece for herself so she could remember what she had in her possession before it was gone to the West forever.

Today was the first day of November 1975. Emil stared out the window and noticed all the leaves had fallen from the trees. He was nervous. He checked his notebook again. He had entered the last entry of his precious possessions he had given to Meyer. He totaled the amount from the receipts they gave him.

He slid back into his chair. His hand was clenched over his mouth to muffle his excitement. "Hooray! I did it!"

Finally, he had paid his entire tax bill—one million Eastern marks. He was finished with the finance department. He was finished with the state dealer. Resting his head on the table, he was relieved the ordeal was over.

Emil maintained a sense of propriety. He worked at the office more often instead of his home. He wanted his boss to see he needed his small-paying job. There were no graphic artists with his skills, so he made sure he let them know how valuable he was to them, especially when higher officials sought him out. He showed them he was a good citizen by attending various meetings and lectures about the regime's good relations with the people regarding their welfare. He hated it, but he had no choice. This was life in the GDR now.

He was aware the ruthless Stasi watched him even more than before. He joked with his friends at the coffee shop that the Stasi had become his newest neighbors, waving to them as they watched him from the window on his way to catch the trolley. He was careful whom he invited to his home. His home was his safe haven. There he was surrounded by love and what he cherished most—his art. For Emil, his life became routine and normal. Normal was the status quo. He laughed at the stupidity of the Stasi but kept it to himself. He did not want to end up in jail again.

When he daydreamed, he imagined himself back in time when Zelda was home. Max was playing outside, and Marie was helping her mother in the kitchen. He could not let go of the loss he felt when his family left for the West. He still shed tears over it.

During his most private moments, he would remember the painful rejection he felt when Max told him he did not want to go back with him to the East. He thought, *I will never forget those words until the day I die.*

Emil realized his indiscretions had cost him dearly. He could not help himself. He loved the attention he got from his beautiful admirers. He never asked; they just offered it. It was his folly. He enjoyed entertaining and mentoring his followers, who wanted to listen and learn about art. He was quite the intellectual, often engaging his students in conversation. They admired him and showered him with affection. He liked being a *Renaissance man*. He never cared about politics or the establishment. He was a lucky man.

It was at this time that he appealed to his inner soul. "I can never change who I am, but I can try to be a better man. I want Max to be proud of me. Wait until he sees the Diesel Museum of Art and Antiquities that I will create one day. Max will have his legacy."

Chapter 34

Early morning light filled the small café. Emil sat, legs stretched out, reading a newspaper with both hands. He glanced at the headlines and the date above it: Wednesday, November 25, 1975. He picked up his coffee and breathed in the steaming aroma. He took a sip, tasting the bold flavor, and followed it with a hearty bite of a spiced muffin. He waved to his friend Otto to join him at the table.

They chatted over the news of the day: "Government fights housing shortages. East Germans build large Plattenbau settlements, blocks of high-rises, in the periphery of Erfurt." They laughed over old memories of the Minor Market—their old cruising ground. It was the small square on the east side of Gera River, framed by early aristocrats and merchants' houses.

Emil got up to put his coat on and wrapped his red scarf around his neck. He fixed his beret so that it slanted to one side and down over his eyes. He was still a handsome man.

After taking a few steps, a sharp pain went through his stomach. He bent over. His eyes winced from the extreme pain. His body flinched as he fell onto the ground. His friend Otto ran to him.

"Emil, what is wrong?" he said. He leaned over him to hear him.

"My stomach . . . it hurts," Emil whispered.

Others rushed to his side. They picked him up and carried him out to one of their cars. They drove him to the nearest hospital's emergency room, where he was placed on a stretcher and wheeled through the doors to be checked. Otto panicked. He had to wait outside.

There were two other men of dubious character waiting outside too. They arrived soon after his friends had brought Emil inside. No one noticed the black van following their car as they drove to the hospital.

Otto called Emil's home. His mother answered the phone.

Holding back his tears, he said, "Emil is in the hospital. He collapsed in the café. Something is wrong with his stomach."

Frieda called Marlene at work to come at once. "It's Emil. We must go to the hospital."

Gustav waited for Marlene then drove them to the hospital. They both held each other's hands tight, too upset to speak.

The doctor came out to talk to them. He told them Emil had ruptured his stomach; it was bleeding. He needed surgery right away. His mother signed the papers. Emil was brought into surgery one hour later.

No one noticed the two strange men in black trench coats following the doctor. No one noticed them whispering in the doctor's ear.

Frieda and Marlene consoled each other. Their despair was uncontrollable. Each one thought only about their fate.

Marlene leaned closer to Frieda. "If Emil does not make it, we must protect the art. We have to take care of ourselves. We must think."

A brief moment of guilt came over them. They could not look at each other.

"We will pray for Emil," said Frieda. "He has survived worse setbacks."

They waited together, barley speaking to each other. Four hours went by as they agonized over their future. The doctor walked over to them with a troubled look on his face. He told them Emil's heart gave out. He did not survive the surgery.

"I am so sorry" was all he could say.

In that moment, shock and disbelief tore through their entire bodies.

Frieda cried out, "Emil is gone? How is this possible? He was feeling so good. It is not supposed to be this way. My son should not die before me."

Marlene tried to comfort her. "We must get home and tell family and friends. We have a lot to prepare."

No one noticed the two suspicious men who followed Frieda and Marlene out the door, nodding in agreement.

When Marlene was home, she called her friend Ernst Ritter. He was a former lawyer and was now a state prosecutor and Stasi informer. She needed Ernst. The news of the death of Emil, an East German art collector, would spread throughout the art world. She called her friend in Berlin.

Frieda, who was in her nineties, was devastated. She called her daughter, Karla, who was able to get a pass to the East from the West. She would come and stay with her mother and help with the arrangements. Marlene called Marie to come and help. She would stay with Marlene. Marie called Zelda in Düsseldorf. Zelda called her son, Max, the sole heir who lived in the States.

Arrangements were made with the help of Karl Gunter, Emil's lawyer and friend. The funeral was to be held on Saturday in a small cemetery outside Erfurt. Frieda and Karla were the first to say goodbye. Marlene and Marie followed. Zelda followed after them. Max was not there to see his father one last time. Other family members paid their respects, along with his close friends from the café and local admirers. Loyal Gustav could not stop crying. Of course, the director of the Gera Museum and the other museum directors and their curators arrived to say farewell to a great collector. Zelda told Emil's dear friend Hans Shulman of his death. He was heartbroken.

The tombstone read "Emil Diesel, born September 12 1911. died November 25 1975. *HIS LIFE BELONGED TO ART.*"

There it was. Emil's fate was now cast in stone. The fate of his art was now at hand.

Part III

Max
1975–2003

Chapter 35

The devastating phone call came at noon on November 25. Max recognized his mother's clear, distinct voice.

"Maximilian, something terrible has happened. I received the call from Marlene. Your father is dead. He died in the hospital in Erfurt. It was his stomach."

Shocked by the news, he felt his knees buckle underneath him, and he sat quickly in his chair.

"I will be there as fast as I can," he said.

"Wait," she interrupted. "You do not have to go to Erfurt. Everything is in such disarray. There is nothing you can do, and there is nothing left to inherit. Whatever Karla and I can get out and turn into cash we will share with you." She was in a hurry to hang up the telephone.

Max was confused. He did not understand what his mother was telling him. Nothing made sense.

"I'll call you back," he said, raising his voice. He gripped the arms of the chair so tight that indentations were left in the leather. His head was throbbing as the pain moved to his eyes. He needed time to think.

Soon the telephone rang again. He hesitated to pick it up and waited for the person to say something first. It was Marie.

"Maximilian, I miss your father so much. I cannot believe he is gone. I must tell you about the conversation I overheard. Karla was talking to your mother just before she called you about your father's death. I heard Karla say these words to your mother: 'Tell him not to come.' Max, do not listen to your mother and aunt. They are lying to you. They want your father's art for themselves. You must come right away. You are the rightful heir."

"Marie, we will talk when I arrive in Erfurt. Then you can tell me everything about my father and his art from the beginning."

There was something bad going on in Erfurt. He had to find out what was happening. Max was annoyed. He could not get a visa until the last day of November. He would miss his father's funeral, and now he must worry about his mother and aunt trying to swindle him out of his inheritance. He was not happy.

Max had not seen his father since 1970. Filled with overwhelming emotions, he remembered the last time they had sat and talked together in East Berlin. He had forgiven his father that day, telling him he would see him again soon. He missed him. There were many times he thought to visit, but he never did. Now it was too late. He would be visiting him at his grave. His father was only sixty-four years old. Max did not expect to be going to East Germany under these circumstances.

In Erfurt, art appeared to vanish from Emil's house. A small figurine was placed in a pocket, and an old book from the library was tucked away under a jacket. Friends and strangers came by the house to express their condolences to Frieda and Karla, only to leave with a souvenir of art under their arms or coats. Marie watched from downstairs as the rooms emptied. One day, someone saw Frieda, as old as she was, running down the street after a friend with a piece of art in her hands. It was ridiculous.

The museum directors came from Erfurt and Dresden. They fought, challenging the finance department in Berlin. This time, there was no way the art that was left was going to the West to pay the remainder of the tax bill. The art was to remain in East Germany and to be divided among the museums. They pleaded their case to the highest levels of the regime to keep the art preserved in the East. This time, they won.

They were like scavengers taking their own private inventory of Emil's collection.

They appraised each item lower in value than before so they could take as much as they could. Each director chose items of interest for their museums. They crated their items and placed them to the side.

The inventory list was given to the state-run gallery to be calculated and applied to Emil's tax bill before they could remove the art they had chosen from the house. There was no mention that Emil had paid his entire bill.

The Gera Museum made sure they acquired the majority of the remaining art collection. Each of the directors held on to their lists. Do not think for one moment that the directors did not help themselves to pieces of art as they walked through the house. Everyone had something in their pockets when they walked out the door.

No one had noticed the small marks on the back of the remaining art that had been left behind. Each museum had left their mark of interest. Once the tax bill was paid, they would be back to pick up the items for their museum. Most of the art left was heavy and large, like the Roman bath and the chinoiserie cabinet.

Marlene told no one about the hidden art she had in storage. Why should she? It was hers now. No one even knew the artifacts were gone, except Emil. He took the secret to his grave. She kept Ernst Ritter close by her side, just in case there was trouble ahead. He had connections high up in the regime. She was so clever and smart to ask Ernst to become her financial adviser.

Marlene had tucked away a list of gifts, including the camel, the ox, and the amphora that Emil had promised her and his mother. The truth was, after Emil's death, Marlene and his mother agreed to make a list of the objects they wanted before the museums came. Since there was no will, they made up the list to look as if Emil had prepared it a while ago. He was known for making notes and lists on pieces of paper and putting them in his pockets and drawers of furniture. They shook hands and promised they would keep the same story.

The list included a gift of 50,000 marks to Gustav, the chauffeur. Marlene had promised him money if he helped her and Frieda remove the items out of the house to a safe place. He was never a good Stasi informer anyway, and he needed the money more. He agreed never to say anything.

She showed the list to Ernst and promised to compensate him well if he would confirm that this list, to be shown to Max and other interested parties, was an accurate account of Emil's last wishes. To protect himself, Ernst had kept records of persons of interest in his network that now included Marlene, and he made sure he was well paid for his time with generous "gifts" of art.

The express train ride to Erfurt was emotional for Max as his thoughts fixated on his father. *I will never see my father again.* He recalled the little Buddha his father had given him in East Berlin but could not take with him. "It was not supposed to end like this for us. This was to be a new beginning," he mumbled under his breath.

He thought about his mother. *If I cannot trust my mother, I am certain I am not going to trust the rest of the family, except for Marie. I can trust her. I will happily accept my inheritance despite the awful past, and I never have to come back here again.*

Papers were cleared at the border in Eisenach. In Erfurt, he went straight to the hotel, left his bags, then took the trolley to his father's house. The show was about to begin.

From the window, Marie was the first to see Max climb the stairs. His feet slammed the cement with each step. His teeth were clenched. He looked angry. She ran to open the door.

She wrapped her arms around him. "Maximilian, it is so good to see you. You cannot imagine what has been going on here."

"I have a good idea, Marie. After talking to my mother, I realized it's not going to be easy for me to get my inheritance without the family wanting their share. How much art is there, Marie?"

"When I arrived for the funeral, there was much more art in the house. At least half is gone," she said. She watched in dismay as anger took over his posture.

He shouted, "Where is the rest of the family? I want to talk to them now!"

To calm him down, Marie brought him a good shot of vodka before he walked with her into the living room. Max walked toward each of them, extending his hand only. He did acknowledge his grandmother with a smile and a hug. He addressed his aunt Karla with a tone of polite indignation. He greeted his cousin Marlene with disdain. He acknowledged Ernst, who had met him at the border in Eisenach, and shook hands with Dr. Hans Brewer, the director of the Gera Museum, whom he had not seen since he was a young boy.

Max sat next to Marie. He drank his vodka, assessing his next move. Everyone was uncomfortable.

An icy feeling filled the room.

Max looked straight at Marlene, trying to calmly articulate in German, "I heard my father's art—no, *my* art—has been leaving this house without my knowledge. I want to know who took it. You were here with my grandmother, so I place the responsibility on you to tell me what happened in this house."

Marlene tried to avert her eyes away from his.

"Max, it has been crazy here since your father died," she said. "There have been so many people in and out of here." She didn't answer the question and tried to change the subject. "I asked Ernst to help with the estate and paperwork. I thought he would be able to help you concerning any matters you have since he was a state prosecutor."

"Thank you, Ernst," Max said. "I am positive I will be needing your advice. Let's meet tomorrow."

Marlene interrupted Max, "The museum directors and curators have been taking inventory and packing crates of art for their museums."

Dr. Brewer glared at her, annoyed that she revealed this. She let him continue talking.

"The finance department agreed to give us the art for our museums, and its value was credited to your father's account to pay his debt. Your father's art could have gone to the West to be sold for currency. We did not want this to happen to your father's collection this time. I know your father would have wanted his art to go to our museum."

Max felt his blood pressure rise and could not resist sarcasm.

"Dr. Brewer, how noble of you to want to see my father's art in your museum. You forget one very important fact: I am the sole heir. I make the decision where my father's collection—my collection—goes. I have not given anyone permission to take anything. Tomorrow I have a meeting with the finance department. I suggest you do not crate any more of my art until you hear from me and the finance department."

Marlene, nodding, signaled to Ernst. She got up and asked if anyone wanted more coffee and cake. Ernst followed her to the kitchen.

"What is happening?"

"Maximilian is no fool. He is suspicious. He wants his inheritance," he whispered. "We may have to help him. Let's see what happens tomorrow at the meeting with the finance department."

Max had heard enough from the director. He was tired and eager to get back to the safe confines of his hotel. He did not want to stay with any of them in his father's house. He kissed his grandmother on the cheek, gave a big hug to Marie, and shook hands with Ernst and Dr. Brewer.

Marlene walked him to the door. "Max, I loved your father. I will help you get your inheritance. Your father did not make a will. He made a small list of gifts to your grandmother, to me, and to Gustav. It was his wish if anything happened to him. I will show you the list later. I know he wanted you to inherit his collection. You are his son. You may not believe me, but he talked about you a lot. He loved you." She kissed him on the cheek.

He walked to the end of the street, thinking, *How am I going to handle this mess?*

Dusk filled the sky as the last ray of sun went down, and he felt the chill in the air through his cashmere vest. When the old red trolley passed by, he hopped on. It stopped at the street where a short walk took him to the small historic hotel.

He realized Erfurt had not changed all that much. The charm was still there, and yet there was an unsettling calm in the air.

Chapter 36

Max was twenty-seven years old when he walked into the state finance department, ready to take a defiant stand regarding his inheritance. All eyes were on him. His handsome demeanor attracted attention right away. He still embodied the youthful German image: tall and lean, silky blond hair, and dark-brown eyes. He flashed a smile at the women with confidence and determination. They succumbed and ran over to welcome this young man, stumbling to see who got there first.

Max might have looked composed, but he was now apprehensive. The head of the department, Dr. Melkus, approached him and extended his hand. Max looked into his eyes with authority and gave him a firm handshake. Then he followed him into his office.

Dr. Melkus spoke with a smug attitude. "Mr. Diesel, you are here to inquire about your father's art collection."

"Yes," Max said. "I want to know why curators from the museums were in my father's house, taking inventory. I was told that my father had paid his entire tax bill before he died. I am sole heir and therefore have sole right to claim my father's art collection through my inheritance. I do not understand why you authorized the museums to take the collection."

Melkus looked past Max, avoiding his gaze.

"You are quite mistaken, Mr. Diesel. Your father still owed 500,000 marks toward his tax debt. Our records show that only 500,000 marks from the sale of your father's art to the state gallery had been applied to his account. We were forced to give the rest of his collection to the Gera Museum and to other museums to settle his outstanding tax debt."

Max's eyes pierced right through Dr. Melkus. He could not contain himself. "I am the sole heir! I did not give permission, verbal or written, for you to give the remainder of my father's art to the museums. I am happy to pay the remainder of my father's debt."

"Not possible! The exchange was final and cannot be challenged." He smirked with a haughty tone.

Max understood things were different here, but not this bad. Melkus was lying. If this case was in the West, he would be able to challenge the claim in court. In the East, he had no rights to fight the Communist system. There was nothing he could do.

He shook his head and remembered the conversation he had with his father's attorney, Dr. Gunter, earlier. He had explained to Max that under East German law, he could not take anything out from the estate to the West. When the debt was paid, any art left over would be sold to the state-run art company and converted into marks, and he would have to pay inheritance and estate taxes on that art. Any money left over was deposited into a bank account established in his name. Each time he would visit, he would be allowed to withdraw fifteen marks a day.

Dr. Gunter confirmed what the attorney in Düsseldorf had told him.

"Don't bother. You won't get your father's art back," the attorney said. "They will manipulate and coerce you, including the law, to achieve their own goals. If you do succeed, Max, let me know how you did it. I could help others in the same situation."

Max did not believe him; naivety got in the way. It seemed there would be no way to reason with the state pawns. He could not hide his disappointment.

"There must be something I can do to gain my inheritance."

"No, I'm sorry." Melkus thanked him for coming in to see him.

Max went straight to the bar at the hotel. He was furious. He had to think; he had to do something. He ordered a beer and thought about his next move. He would go to see Ernst. Ernst understood manipulation and coercion. After all, he was a state prosecutor. He did tell him he wanted to help him.

That evening, Max had an invitation to dinner from one of his father's friends, Dr. Voigt. Years ago, Voigt had helped him, his mother, and Marie leave East Germany. He hugged Max for a long time and was pleased to see what a fine young man he had become.

"Your father would be proud," he said, his eyes filling with tears.

During dinner, Voigt asked Max if much art had been stolen from the house, asking specifically about several eighteenth-century porcelain figurines that he had been interested in.

"I did not see any of those pieces," he said.

Max realized everybody was more interested in his father's art than his father.

The next day, Max called Ernst after breakfast. "I am on my way to the house. Meet me in fifteen minutes."

"Okay," he said. Ernst called Marlene and told her to be there to greet him. She opened the door for Max and kissed him on the cheek.

"Max, I am so glad you are here. Ernst is on his way," she said. Marlene poured him a cup of coffee in the kitchen.

He looked at her, thinking his cousin was still a fine-looking woman. She was not that much older than himself.

He remembered the day she had come to the West to see his mother. He had been twenty with a well-developed ego and had tried to make a pass at her. He had kissed her and placed his hand underneath her skirt, moving it until his fingers had touched her silk panty. With both hands on his chest, she had pushed him away. "Max, I am with your father now. We can't do this," she had said. He had let go of her, feeling a little rejected, then laughed at the thrill of the chase. She must have been reading his mind because she had smiled and laughed at him.

Ernst walked in and sat at the table, puffing on a cigarette. Max told them about his meeting at the finance department. Ernst already knew the outcome of the meeting.

Max's voice got louder as his temper flared. "I will fight for my inheritance. It's mine," Max said.

Ernst winked at Marlene as he took another puff of his cigarette. "Max, take it easy," Ernst said. "You don't want to make any trouble for yourself and for everyone involved. There is another way. I will arrange for you to get ten percent of the art collection from the museum's list."

Max was stunned. "You want to make a deal?"

"I know ten percent does not sound like a lot, but it is better than nothing. I can persuade the department to let ten percent go. I will tell them ninety percent is staying in the East. That is an attractive offer for them. They do not want trouble with Berlin. Now there are a few conditions. You have to do something for us," he said.

Marlene pulled out of her pocket Emil's list, the one she had prepared, which gave her and his grandmother gifts from his collection and the 50,000 marks she had promised Gustav.

"You must agree to honor the list of gifts your father made to Marlene and to your grandmother, including 50,000 marks to Gustav. Second, you must agree to never say anything about art leaving the house after your father passed away. We know art was stolen. There is no way to get it back. Let us just leave it at that. Third, you must never talk to anyone regarding those who helped you take your art out of East Germany."

"Wow," Max said. "You really are asking me to make a deal with you. That's called a bribe."

"It depends on how one looks at it," he said, laughing under his breath. "Max, you want something. I want something. It is as simple as that. I can make it happen."

"If I say okay, I want to be able to choose the art," Max said. "Also, I want one important piece—the cabinet that is in the living room."

Nothing was written down. It was a clear verbal agreement. Max and Ernst shook hands. Marlene sealed it with a kiss. He walked back to the hotel, dazed by it all.

He could not believe it! He was so young. What did he know about deceit? Nothing! He had to agree with the plan because he knew too much and the art was rightfully his. Marlene and Ernst had conspired together to set this plan in motion.

"Go home, Max. I will call you when it is time for you to come again," Ernst said.

Max was ready to leave the East. He called home that evening. He told Helga he was taking the train to Frankfurt and would be back home in the States the next day.

Chapter 37

Helga took one look at his disheveled appearance and knew his trip had been difficult for him.

Exhausted, he kept his story short. "Helga, I am still upset about my father's death. I never got a chance to tell him I was sorry I stayed away so long. Now it is too late.

She put her arms around him. "I'm so sorry, Max."

He buried his head on her shoulder, relieved that she did not pressure him to talk further. He had no intention of telling her the real reason why he was so upset.

"I will have to go back to Erfurt because the estate is not settled," he said. He did not mention anything else to her.

"I want to go back with you next time," she said. "I want to pay my respects to your grandmother and Marie."

Max thought it was a good idea. She was an American citizen, and it would make his arrival less conspicuous.

Christmas was a good distraction. Celebrations were happening everywhere. Max enjoyed spending time with his friends. Everyone loved his loud voice with the German accent and his bold German personality to match. He entertained them with his quick wit, dry humor, and great stories about his travels. His friends were always telling him what a fun guy he was. He was the life of the party. Like his father, his charisma and charm were addictive. They showered him with attention, feeding his ego, especially when he talked about himself. Max thought he was a handsome, classy guy. Girls competed for his attention, which was not great for his wife, who was always flying somewhere.

One day, he had worked late. The drive to the South Shore was not easy in the wintertime. He was glad he had a place to stay with friends when he was too tired to drive home. His wife was on a trip, and he did not like to be alone.

That night, he lay sprawled out on the bed. Sweaty and hot, he pushed the blanket to one side, thinking about his next visit to the East. He asked Ernst why he was taking so long to prepare his claim to the finance department. In Erfurt, his attorney told him he had only one year to make his case. He had a hunch Ernst was stalling.

He twisted the sheet tight the more he thought about what Ernst had said: "Relax. You worry too much. I have control of the entire situation. Be patient."

Max was not a patient man. Patience was not in his DNA.

"When the holidays are over, I will be seeing you in Erfurt," Max said.

New Year's Eve was uneventful. Helga had to fly over the holiday. Again, Max did not have his wife with him to celebrate, but it did not stop him from celebrating. He had many invitations to neighborhood parties. Laughter, good drinks, and great conversation made forgetting his wife easy. The evening was not a disappointment after all. Nineteen seventy-six arrived with little fanfare. Max woke up late, and Helga was in her bed, asleep in the next room.

Chapter 38

In Erfurt, Dr. Brewer was uneasy. He tried to cover his shaking hands beneath the table as he sat across from his wife during dinner in his home. He could not get out of his head the look of disappointment Max had on his face when he last saw him at his father's house.

"Hans, what is wrong with you?" she said.

"Maximilian, poor bastard. He really got screwed out of his inheritance," he said. "We have known the Diesel family all our lives. Emil was a true artist and a passionate collector. His death was a tragedy for all of us. It is a mockery that his son was denied his inheritance." Guilt consumed him when he thought about Max's plight. "He is a wonderful young man." His eyes turned toward the two hand-colored books on the bookshelf. He had slipped them into his pockets from Emil's library. "These books were gifts from Emil," he said, quickly brushing aside his moment of shame.

Meanwhile, at home, Ernst finished preparing all the documents. He had to make sure he had stamped seals of approval from the finance department, and the Gera Museum on each one. There was very little sleep for him that night as he went over each detail in his head. There could not be any mistakes.

The next day, he met with Dr. Brewer.

"Hans, we are going to release to Max ten percent of the remaining art left in the house. I want you to decide for him which art he should take. Also, I want him to have the Chinese cabinet. I do not care how you make that happen. Make a list of the items that he will take with him with the appraisal amounts. Ten percent is not a large amount, considering what you are getting. And there still is plenty of art left for you to take after Max leaves with his share. Do we understand each other?" Ernst said.

Hans nodded. "I understand."

Later that day, Ernst met with Dr. Melkus at the finance department. Ernst knew he would agree to his proposal. He was at the house when they took the inventory the second time. He saw Melkus help himself to a few pieces of art on his way out the door. He would offer other gifts he could not refuse if he had to encourage him a little more.

"Melkus, I think it would be a good idea to give Maximilian Diesel ten percent of the remaining art left in the house. He is not a patient young man. He can be foolish and cause trouble for all of us. We don't have to be greedy. Anyway, what is left will go to the museums. I need your stamp of approval releasing the art to him on all documents. Once you have the list, you can prepare the tax document he needs so that he can settle his inheritance and estate taxes. I want to have this case with Maximilian Diesel handled with no mistakes."

Agitated, Dr. Melkus agreed with Ernst. He was not going to take a chance and argue with a state prosecutor. He had too much power at the state level. He could end up behind bars or, worse, dead. Ernst left his office quite satisfied.

His dealing with Berlin was the easiest. He had reminded his contacts in the culture and finance departments that it would be wise for them to agree to allow Maximilian to take 10 percent of art to the West. In return, the East would keep 90 percent. Only then would each of them be compensated. They were hungry for the money.

He explained clearly, so they understood.

"Max is only interested in the monetary value of the art. I have made sure that once Max sells his art in the West, he would send me a specified amount of hard currency from his sales back to me. I have agreed to share the money with you."

His plan was ready to be executed. He had everyone in place.

Before Max returned to Erfurt, he would have made secure arrangements for police security at the house and would have arranged for an official government transport truck, a driver, and security guards. He hoped Max would not be difficult. If this deal was to be successful, everyone had to do their part and keep quiet about it.

Chapter 39

In February 1976, Max and Helga flew into Frankfurt. They didn't sit together because the flight was full, and flying standby with a free pass in first-class did not always guarantee seats together.

Max was glad they were sitting in separate seats this time. He was nervous as hell. He did not know what to expect once he arrived in Erfurt. The less his wife knew about his inheritance, the better. He did not want her involved in this deal he had made with Ernst and Marlene.

They took the train to Erfurt. The snow on the tracks slowed the train's speed as it passed through the sleepy towns of Germany. At each stop, the train picked up passengers bundled up in heavy wool coats. Plain-colored scarves wrapped tightly around their necks covered their mouths and ears. Fur hats, wool berets, and suede hats with ears covered their heads so much only their eyes peeked through. Some people snoozed; others read or chatted quietly together. Everything appeared normal, but this was East Germany. Weren't they afraid too?

Studying people was one of his favorite pastimes. In the summer, he loved sitting outside a café, sipping a double espresso and watching the people go by. He was amused at how many of them walked by, eating pretzels with mustard, pastries filled with cream, and ice cream. They held their food in one hand and talked with the other. Even though it was winter, people still licked their gelato cones as they stepped carefully with heavy tread boots on the snowy ground.

No one seemed to care or notice the change in the air.

When they arrived at the border in Eisenach, everybody had to exit the train. Ernst met them at the train station. He waved to Max when he caught his attention.

"Come this way," he said. Ernst took their passports and went into a small cubicle called the office. He motioned Max and his wife to wait. Ernst approached them and handed their passports with their visas back to them.

"You can pass through now and continue to Erfurt," he said. Each showed their visa to the officer. Both visas were only good for a week, but Ernst would get an extension for Max's visa for another three weeks, just like before.

Max remembered being anxious the first time Ernst took his passport. He pulled his hand away because he felt threatened. His lifeline to the West was taken away from him. He did not like that uncomfortable feeling. This time, it was easier because he knew Ernst was on his side. This man knew all the right people and had many connections high up in the regime.

Max and Ernst shook hands. He introduced Ernst to Helga as a close friend of his father's and Marlene. She smiled back. She couldn't wait to board the train to Erfurt. She was tired and eager to go to the hotel, wanting to rest and freshen up before she met Max's grandmother and Marlene. Most of all, she wanted to enjoy this trip with Max and hoped they could rekindle their marriage vows.

Ernst got his car and drove them to their hotel. The manager welcomed Max back and offered him a beer from the bar. He had grown fond of the bar. He liked to unwind with a scotch before retiring and looked forward to having that drink again.

Max had arranged to meet at his father's house so that his wife could spend time with Frieda. She was growing old and did not want to leave the house during the winter months. Despite her age, her memory was sharp, and she remained vigilant. Marlene had made dinner reservations at a restaurant near the house for the three of them.

Marlene greeted Max at the door with a hug. She kissed Helga on each cheek. "It is wonderful you could come with Max. He won't feel so lonely this time." His wife wondered what Marlene meant by that remark.

She walked straight to Frieda and gave her a big hug, saying, "I am sorry for your loss. Emil was too young to die. He was a brilliant artist." They sat down on the sofa together and chatted away for a long time in German.

Meanwhile, Max and Marlene had found their way to the kitchen. She poured the vodka into small shot glasses. They raised their glasses to toast the future.

Max tried to lower his voice. "I don't want Helga to hear. She doesn't know anything. I told her I had to sign more papers to settle the estate."

He drummed his fingers on the table. "Marlene, this is taking a long time."

"Dear Max, paperwork takes so long these days. Ernst knows what he is doing. Patience, handsome! You are meeting him in a few days. He will tell you what to do."

He still felt uneasy. He did not like being blindsided.

Max was ready to meet with Ernst. He was anxious, eager to get his art, and run with it to the West.

At dinner, Marlene announced some interesting news. Frieda would be moving for good to the West when the snow was gone. She would live with her daughter, Karla, and her son-in-law. After all, she was in her nineties, and she felt she was too old to stay alone in the house. Also, the East Germans would love to get rid of her so they wouldn't have to give her financial support anymore.

"The other big news is, I'm getting married." She was beaming. "I have known my fiancé for a long time. He restores art, too, and works on many projects with me. Also, he gives lectures for the culture department. I will be moving to Berlin in early spring."

"It sounds so romantic," Helga said. She thought how wonderful it was for Marlene to have found a good man during these difficult times under the constraints of the German Democratic Republic.

Max was curious. He sensed she must have an idea when he will get his art. She was covering herself, just in case the deal does not go as planned. *Smart girl.*

Max and Marlene shared stories with Helga about their childhood, living one floor apart. Those were better times in Erfurt when the families were all together. No one wanted to talk about the unhappy times. Max saw Helga yawning and decided to end the evening on a pleasant note.

It had been a long time since they shared a bed together. Their schedules often conflicted because of her work. Max held her tight, and she responded just the way he wanted her to. She fell sound asleep in his arms.

He lay there, still and silent, in the darkness. He could not sleep. Too many thoughts were running through his mind. His naked body trembled at the thought of having to trust the word of Ernst and Marlene. He dared not open his eyes. He did not want it to be real; he wanted it gone.

Chapter 40

Dr. Brewer spent several days at the house, making a list of the remaining art that Max would choose for himself—with his help, of course. The list added up to 10 percent. He made a second list too. This list contained the pieces of art that had been marked by the museum directors. Their art would be picked up after Max took his share out of East Germany.

Dr. Brewer appraised his list very low to give Max more so he would feel he was compensated well for his 10 percent. Max was young and impulsive, and he did not know or appreciate the value of the art. He anticipated that Max would sell his art in the West right away. He had to satisfy everyone. There could not be any hint of trouble.

Max met Ernst on the fourth day. "You're stalling," said Max.

"No, Max. I keep telling you it takes time to prepare the documents for approval. We do not want to make any mistakes," he said, firing the words back at him.

Deep down, Max was not convinced, but he gave in anyway.

Ernst was determined to resolve any doubts. "Next week you will meet Dr. Brewer at your father's house. He will help you select the art you will take to the West."

Max's defenses went up. "I want to choose the pieces."

Ernst was concerned, knowing Max could be stubborn and obsessive and could do something they all might regret.

"It should not be a problem. Dr. Brewer will advise you. After you have finished choosing the objects, Max, *you will go home.* I will take care of the legalities. When you return, your art will be packed up and ready to leave the East."

Max felt his legs stiffen as he took a guarded stance. "How do I know you are telling me the truth? There is no way you can get the art over the border. There are armed guards everywhere," Max said.

Ernst was indignant. "You little shit. Remember I am doing you a favor. If it wasn't for me, you would get nothing."

Startled, Max's posture changed. He sat still, hands folded in front of him, resolved to keep his mouth shut and eyes focused on the floor.

Ernst looked at the pitiful figure before him. He was hard on him and felt a little guilty. Ernst had so much to gain—both art and currency. He regained his composure and tried a different tactic.

"Max, I am going to show you how much power I have in the regime. I will convince you the deal I presented to you will work."

"Show me," Max said.

"Your wife leaves in a few days to go back to the West."

"That is correct. She will stay with my mother in Düsseldorf."

"I am going to have her train make an unscheduled stop. This train is an interzone train. It starts in Berlin and makes stops in the major cities, like Leipzig and Erfurt. It stops at the border then continues on to Düsseldorf." He leaned forward. "Station guards will enter the train and look for your wife. They will escort her off the train. She will be placed on another train to Düsseldorf. She will not be harmed or interrogated. They will treat her very well. Will this satisfy your doubts about the power that I have in the regime?"

"I believe it will," Max said. His voice quivered.

He could not mention this event to anybody, especially Helga. Two days later, his wife packed her suitcase and said goodbye to Max. He did not want Helga to travel alone and arranged for her to travel with an older woman friend of his grandmother. His wife was pleased because she didn't feel safe traveling through East Germany by herself to the West.

Max was worried about all this. His nerves were overtaking his usually assertive demeanor. He was a realist and did not like the odds.

After all, this was the GDR. He would sit by the telephone and wait for Helga's call.

Meanwhile, Helga chatted away in perfect German with the gray-haired woman in her flannel dress, which she had made herself. Halfway through their conversation, her companion dozed off. She could feel herself nodding off from the motion of the train. Instead of resting, she became engrossed in her book. It was going to be a long, tiring train ride. After a few hours, she closed her sleepy eyes. All of a sudden, the train came to a complete stop. She peeked out the window. It was dusk, and the station appeared deserted.

She gently tapped her companion's shoulder. "I wonder why we are stopping."

"I have no idea."

Curious now, she looked out the window and all around.

The train's doors opened. Five tall, inquisitive security guards in gray uniforms walked through the train. They held a picture in their hands. They were looking for a passenger.

Helga whispered, "They are looking for someone."

One of the guards motioned to the others. They stopped in front of Helga's seat. He politely asked Helga for her papers. "You are Helga Diesel?"

"Yes, I am." She was frightened. Her hands shook as she handed the papers to the guard.

"Please come with us, Mrs. Diesel. Do not worry. No harm will come to you," he said. The guards escorted her off the train.

She followed them to a small well-lit office the size of a cubicle inside the station. They told her to wait. No explanation was given. They gave her black coffee and a little pastry filled with raspberry jam. She did not dare ask any questions. This was uncharted territory for her. Aware of her nervousness, they tried to be pleasant and asked her if she enjoyed her stay in East Germany. They assured her she would be boarding the next train when it arrives. One hour later, the train arrived. They gave back her papers and passport, thanked her for her patience, and put her on the train.

When her companion arrived in Düsseldorf, she called Zelda and told her what had happened to Helga.

"They just came in and took her off the train." She was upset and told Zelda to call her the moment she heard from Helga.

An hour later, a frazzled Helga arrived at Zelda's house.

"You won't believe what has happened to me," she said, bewildered by the chain of events she had just experienced.

"I know. Frieda's friend called me. Are you okay?"

"Yes, it was the strangest thing. They looked at my papers, gave me coffee, and put me on the next train. They did not even question me."

"Call Max right away. He will be worried," Zelda said.

Her account of her story to Max was full of drama.

"I'm fine, but I'm exhausted," she said. "They put me on the next train. Wait! Max, wait! I am watching the news on the television. They just mentioned how the interzone train made an unscheduled stop today."

Max called Ernst the next day. "You're hired!" he said.

"Max, don't worry anymore. I will talk to Dr. Brewer and let you know what day he wants to meet you at your father's house."

Chapter 41

Max met Dr. Brewer at his father's house on Tuesday. Somber, Max walked through the half-empty house. There was still so much art left—paintings, sculptures, large furniture, and more. He was baffled. He could not comprehend how his father had acquired such a massive art collection. He assumed the collection must have been worth millions. To think that more than half had been sold to pay his father's tax debt and now stolen and confiscated made him furious. The worst of it was, he could do nothing about it. He was backed into a corner, and there was no way out except to go with the plan if he wanted his inheritance, no matter how small it was.

Hans showed him the list he had prepared. He pointed out the items as they walked through each room. Max recognized some of them—the modern painting by the drunken artist, Diesse, whom his father had supported, and the hand-painted beer stein that sat on the side table in the library. He wanted those items. Other pieces acquired by Emil were unfamiliar because Max had moved to the West with his mother.

Max agreed to most of the items Hans showed him, but there were more specific items he wanted, like the bronzes of the lion and the tiger and the fine bronze head of Buddha, its face depicting a state of meditation. He remembered seeing them growing up. He knew it was very important for him to hold on to those memories, good or bad.

He reminded Dr. Brewer that the German Chinese-style chest was going with him. Brewer's stomach twisted a little. He knew Dresden was interested in the piece. It was appraised ridiculously low so he could show the finance department that the piece was of little interest and not as valuable as they had once thought. He had to convince the finance department since they were responsible for the final approval.

When the list was complete, Brewer had let Max take the pieces he had wanted.

Later, Max met with Ernst. "It's done."

"Now I want you to go home and stop worrying about the details. I will call you when it's time to come back," Ernst said.

"Don't keep me waiting. I cannot keep leaving my job for weeks at a time. Otherwise, I may not have one when I get back."

"Max, the next time will be brief. The transport of your art will move very fast once it is set into motion. I want this over as much as you do." Ernst realized that this was not going to be an easy task. He had to take precautions to make sure everyone worked together.

The next day, Ernst took Max to the train station. They shook hands on their verbal agreement. Both of them walked away from each other, well aware of the high risks involved.

Max arrived in Düsseldorf that evening. His wife had left. Work had called her back, and she couldn't wait for him any longer. His mother tried to get information from him about the estate. He was evasive and short-tempered with her. He could not help it. He could not stop thinking about how his mother, his aunt, Marlene, and his grandmother helped themselves to his share of the inheritance.

In the morning, Max flew back to the States. He was relentless, calling Ernst every week. Ernst continued to tell Max not to worry.

"Soon, very soon," he would say.

Weeks became months. Max was in agony; his patience was growing thin.

One afternoon, Max got the call.

"Max, it's time," Ernst said. "Everything is set to move the second week in April. Come a few days before the move because papers have to be signed and taxes have to be paid by you to the finance department."

Max was thrilled to have this ordeal over with. He did his research. He prepared to sell some pieces of art at auction, as well as to dealers in

West Germany. The money would help him buy some things he needed and help settle some debt.

Ernst had all the required papers for the government transport truck, ready to go. He had signatures from Dr. Hans Brewer, director of the Gera Museum; Dr. Melkus, in charge of the Erfurt's finance department; and himself, Ernst Ritter, as overseer of the Emil Diesel estate. There were also signatures from the state culture department and the customs department. The papers were sealed. The envelope was stamped with their official seals. The driver would hand the envelope over to the guards at the border before entering West Germany.

Ernst told Max that the documents state that Maximilian Diesel, sole heir, has government approval to take possession of his father's art as part of his inheritance.

Max arrived a few days before the move, just as Ernst told him to do. He left his bags at the same hotel and went straight to Ritter's office. When he saw him, Max grew more apprehensive. Ernst seemed a little on edge. He was sitting behind his desk, tapping the top of his pen up and down.

"What now?"

"Oh, it really is nothing, a small favor I have to ask of you," Ernst said.

"What favor?" he said.

"After you go to the state art dealer to sell your art to settle your taxes, I would like you to go to the intershop where only foreigners with hard currency are allowed to buy goods. I have a list of items I would like you to buy for me and for others."

Max took the list off the table and read it. The list was itemized: a color TV for Melkus, a watch for Ritter, wine for Brewer, and the list went on. His face flushed. He lost control.

"I can't afford these things! I don't make that kind of money from my job!"

"Max, I know you have credit cards. Take them to the store. Use your Diners Club card."

Max was shocked. "I can't."

"Of course, you can. I will be there to help you carry out the goods. One more thing. When you arrive in the West, you will not tell anybody where you got your art. If you go to the radio and TV stations and implicate the GDR and me regarding the transport of your new acquisitions, your inheritance, out of the East, we will find you. We know where you live at 23 Mayfair Road, Gateshead, MA."

Max was terrified. "I never told you where I live."

"It does not matter. We have agents everywhere."

Max had a hunch Ernst was an informant for the Stasi. His threat confirmed it.

"One more thing, Max. When you arrive in the West, I want you to send me fifty thousand West German marks, which translates into half a million East German marks. You will make money from the sale of your art. When you have the cash in your hands, *you will bring it to me*. We will meet at the border like before."

Max felt nauseous. His entire body stiffened under the pressure. He wiped the sweat from his forehead with his arm. There was no way out. He did the only thing he could. He agreed. He looked straight into Ernst's sinister eyes. His hand was shaking as he took his handshake.

Chapter 42

It was Sunday. Max lay in bed at the hotel until he felt the warmth from the sun all around him. He opened the window, breathing in the fresh, crisp air. Trees were budding, and he could hear people walking outside on the cobblestone sidewalk from his room. He missed hearing the church bells ringing in the morning. Some churches still held a quiet, simple mass on Sunday, but the Communists did not advocate religion and frowned upon church participation.

He kept obsessing about the demands and threats Ernst had made against his life. Feeling insecure only confused him. He didn't like it—not being in control. More than ever, he wanted to get his art out of East Germany and hoped there would be no more surprises.

Max went over the list in his head at breakfast: Monday morning, go to finance department to pay inheritance and estate taxes; afternoon, go to intershop; and Tuesday morning, meet Ernst to review transport of art. He had to make sure he checked out of the hotel first and not forget to buy his train tickets on Monday.

He was so caught up in his thoughts that he didn't eat any of his dark rye bread and cold cuts. He finished his coffee, sighed, and pushed himself from the table in disgust. It was too late now to back out of the deal.

He walked over to the house, expecting the worst. He kept glancing over his shoulder to see if the Stasi were still following him. They had been his constant shadow since his arrival in Germany. They never approached him even when he would run into a small alley on occasion to lose them. They always kept a safe distance.

He thought, *Are they watching me or protecting me?*

His grandmother had left for the West when warmer temperatures dried the streets. His father's house was empty except for the packed crates. The largest pieces of sculpture and vases had been left behind as well as the Roman marble stone baptismal bath that weighed tons. He was alone. He walked through the house, looking to see if there was anything the museums had missed. He found two hand-painted miniatures behind a large vase on the floor. He put them in one of his crates by the door, leaving the other packed crates and the rest of the art behind for the scavengers.

He knew he was lucky to get this much out of East Germany.

Downstairs, he knocked on Marlene's door. She saw it was Max through the peephole, and she opened the door.

Max had a dreadful look on his face. She tried to humor him, saying, "In two more days, you will have your art, and you will be singing a happy tune in the West."

"At what price, Marlene?" He was thinking about the demands Ernst had placed on him.

"Don't worry, Max. This is the East. We all have to survive. I will be leaving the end of the week for Berlin. I have a new life waiting for me."

Her beautiful face was gleaming. She was thinking of her own wonderful inheritance from Emil that was waiting for her there, having moved it from Erfurt to Berlin. Emil would never realize how generous he had been to her. *What a pity!*

She shifted her body so that her knee touched Max's knee. She reached over and slid her hand over his thigh. It aroused him.

"Marlene, what are you doing to me? This is not going to happen. It can't happen. Remember what Ernst said—no mistakes. And there is Helga to consider."

She pulled her hand away, laughed, and neatened herself. She gave Max a quick kiss on the cheek. Then she stood up, winked at him, and walked away.

They said their goodbyes and wished each other well.

Chapter 43

Max woke up early. "Ah, I love spring." This time he breathed in the fresh, crisp air to clear his head. He was ready to take on the day after a hearty breakfast and good, strong coffee. He sprinted to the finance department. The sun felt good on his body. He wanted to be the first one in line to pay his taxes. Dr. Melkus shook hands with Max and told his assistant he would take care of Mr. Diesel himself. Max followed him into his office and sat down across from him. After this meeting, he hoped he would never see him again.

Max was blown away by his attitude. Dr. Melkus thanked him for his patience and told him he was one lucky boy because not everyone got this kind of opportunity these days. He handed Max the tax bill covering the items that he had received from his inheritance and the estate. Max looked over the bill. He did not say a word. He just smiled.

He wiped the beads of sweat from his forehead, sighing with relief as he walked out the door, muttering, "That wasn't so bad." Next stop was the intershop. He looked over the list that Ernst had given him. At the intershop, without any resistance, he read the list to a salesgirl, who placed each item on the counter; the larger item, the TV, was placed on the floor. He noticed Ernst waiting outside and called him in to help carry the purchases out when he had finished signing the receipt.

Ernst patted him on the back. "Good job. Everything is here."

It took three trips for them to carry everything to the white van. Ernst secured the door. "Lunch is on me," he said.

They had this behind them. Everything was on schedule.

During lunch, Ernst discussed tomorrow's plan in detail with Max. "Meet me at the house at nine o'clock. Dr. Brewer will not be there. When the government transport truck arrives, hired workers will carry your crates out of the house and into the truck. I will have security guards in the house and outside the front of the house, where the truck will be. Make sure you are ready to leave right away after the truck is loaded.

"The driver will hand you a receipt for goods received—goods that will be driven to the destination on the receipt. Sign it. The receipt will be handed to the guards at the border, along with the official papers already signed and sealed. You can leave for the train station once you sign the packing slip and receipt.

"Max, you're on your own once you arrive in the West. Good luck, and remember what I told you about keeping quiet. I will see you tomorrow."

Max finished his beer and stood up from the table. "Thanks for lunch, Ernst. I'll see you tomorrow." Max had the rest of the day to think about tomorrow. His stomach was in knots, and he was nervous again.

Ernst felt sorry for Max and called him later that afternoon. "Max, you looked so stressed at lunch. I called the others to meet us at the bar for vodka, champagne, and caviar tonight."

"Great. I didn't feel like being alone."

One last time, Marlene, Hans, Ernst, and Max let their guards down for a moment and, like old friends, toasted to a successful campaign.

Tuesday morning came fast. Max couldn't remember if he closed his eyes at all. He slept fitfully all night, worrying about today. He kept affirming to himself, "Nothing can go wrong today. Stay focused and don't panic." He was desperate for coffee. Breakfast was not appealing. Toast, butter, and jam were all he wanted.

He went back to his room and packed. He checked his train tickets one more time and paid the hotel bill at the front desk. He looked at his watch. Ernst was waiting. Max sprinted up the street and caught the trolley passing by. He couldn't believe it was finally going to be over. He never dreamed he could get his father's art out of Erfurt. He wished he could have taken it all. After all, it was his rightful inheritance. The thought of it going to the museums made his stomach twist. The trolley stopped at the beginning of the street. He hopped off, eyes focused on the sidewalk. The brisk walk was clearing his head.

He looked up. "Damn, I almost passed my house. It's time."

He took a deep breath. With vigor and determination, he double-stepped up to the front door. The door was open. What did this mean? A fearful Max stepped into the house. Three large crates sat in the middle of the room. The German chinoiserie chest was taken apart in three sections: the bottom, the middle, and the top. The chest had its own packing slip that had to be signed.

Ernst was sweating. He wiped the sweat with the sleeve of his shirt.

"Ernst, a little nervous?" Max asked.

"No, no, Max. I don't like waiting. That's all."

Max thought that his response was strange. It was Ernst who always told him to be patient whenever he had difficulty waiting. Ernst made him nervous. The armed security guards standing throughout the house made him nervous. Now he did not feel safe. There had to be at least ten of them. They stood very still and watched. They kept watching. Their eyes kept moving from one corner of the room to the other, then to him and to Ernst.

"Don't worry, Max. They are here to make sure nothing leaves this house except your crates."

The transport truck arrived one hour late. The customs agent arrived behind the truck. Three guards hurried out of the house to secure the truck. Max was standing by the front door. The driver jumped down and walked over to him. The short, sour-faced, pushy customs agent followed, maneuvering himself in front of the driver.

"The driver and his men will carry your crates out to the truck and transport them to the border. After the papers are checked and approved, another driver will continue to take them to Düsseldorf in the West." The driver showed Max a freight slip to look over.

"Sign at the line if this is the correct address where the shipment will be delivered and received." The address was his mother's house in Düsseldorf, and he was the receiver.

Ernst gave the paperwork to the customs agent. He looked over the description of the items written down and stopped at the description of the large cabinet.

"I was told this item was not supposed to go on the truck. It is too valuable, and it is to stay in the East."

Max interrupted with his loud voice, "You are wrong. Dr. Brewer told me I could take my father's chest because it was not as valuable as was first thought by the curators. Look how low the appraisal is."

The customs agent looked around. "Where is Dr. Brewer? I will not authorize the transport of the cabinet until I talk to him."

"Max, call Dr. Brewer," Ernst said.

Max ran to the telephone and made the call. Dr. Brewer was not answering the telephone. Max slammed the phone down, bolted out the back door into the middle of the street, and ran down the narrow side streets. He kept glancing back to make sure no one saw him arrive at Dr. Brewer's front door. Max placed his finger on the bell and left it there.

"Dr. Brewer, Dr. Brewer, answer the door. For my sake, please come to the door."

He heard Max's voice in a panic. He cracked open the door.

"Hans, you better get over to my house right away. They won't release the cabinet unless you are there to sign for it."

"I will get my jacket and drive over. You leave first, and I will see you at the house in ten minutes."

Hans Brewer saw his fate flash before his eyes. He was frantic and talking to himself. "No one will notice or care once it's gone. The curators have enough art."

It was true. Dresden had adjusted the amount of the appraisal low. They got greedy. He tried to tell them it was too low. He couldn't tell them Max wanted it.

He made sure he parked away from the transport truck, knowing it would not be easy to walk past the truck. He stumbled up the stairs and fell into Max as he opened the door.

"Take it easy, Dr. Brewer. No need to rush. You must not create any suspicion."

Ernst hid in the kitchen. The customs agent approached Dr. Brewer and pulled him aside.

"Mr. Diesel tells me you released the cabinet for him to take to the West. I thought it was to stay here."

Brewer spoke as if it was a trivial matter. "It was valued very low, so I decided it couldn't be important anymore. Therefore, I felt there was no reason for me not to let Mr. Diesel take it with him." He signed the receipt. This satisfied the customs agent.

Each crate was placed on the truck with care. The security guards watched with guns in their hands to make sure there was no one in or around the truck.

Max joked, "Are you sure there is no one hiding in the truck counting on a free ride to the West?" No one laughed.

Max stood on the sidewalk, watching his inheritance being driven away. The customs agent followed the truck. He still had misgivings about Ernst and wondered if the truck would make an unscheduled stop on its way to the West. As anxious as he was, he had to take one more leap of faith. He would arrive in Düsseldorf tonight, ready to accept his fortune.

Max shook hands with Dr. Brewer and Ernst Ritter. "Thank you. We did it."

"Remember, Max, I will be waiting to hear from you soon," Ernst said.

"I won't forget."

"Good luck."

Max turned back one more time and stopped. He needed to look again at the grand house where he grew up. Memories flooded his mind. He pictured his father with a scarf wrapped around his neck, a beret tilted over his eyes, and that signature flirtatious smile on his face.

He felt the tears well in his eyes. He did not want to think about him anymore. He was exhausted. All this commotion was a little too much for him to take. He caught the trolley at the top of the street and headed back to the hotel to pick up his bags. He needed to relax and to forget, thinking this was all a crazy dream.

The train was two hours late. He was glad he had bought a reserved ticket for a compartment rather than an open seat. All he wanted to do was sleep and eat. He grabbed a sandwich at the fast-food stand. Later, he would have dinner on the train.

The train screeched to a halt. It was the same train his wife took to go to the West. Only this time, it would not make any unauthorized stops. When it stopped at the border, papers were checked. He let out a huge sigh. "It's over." It was a smooth ride all the way to Düsseldorf.

He arrived at his mother's door late at night. The eight-hour trip was always long and tiring. His mother greeted him with a hug and showed him to the bed she had made up for him. They would talk in the morning.

He woke up to the smell of brewed coffee. In a T-shirt and shorts, he sat across from his mother at the kitchen table. She prepared buttered toast with ham and cheese. She was going out of her way to be kind to him. He wanted to believe she was sincere. Maybe she realized her mistakes and was trying to make amends.

"Mother, a transport truck is due to arrive here between 10:00 and 11:00 a.m. We need to clear the back room because all the crates will be stacked in there for now."

"I will help you."

"I am going to call Rudi to help me bring the crates up to the apartment." Rudi had become a good friend to Max through the years. He was four years older and worked for one of the newspapers in Düsseldorf.

Max had some tense moments of doubt as he waited for the truck. He hoped the truck had cleared the border with the shipment intact. He pulled the curtains back from the window and saw the truck pull into the driveway. The driver honked his horn. Max looked at his watch and laughed. The truck had arrived exactly on time!

He met the driver outside the apartment and signed for the shipment. He still could not believe his art had made it all the way to Düsseldorf from Erfurt without any trouble. Rudi, Max, and the driver carried each crate upstairs to the apartment and stacked them into the back room. Max slipped the driver some marks for his help.

Max and Rudi sat down to enjoy a beer or two. Max thanked him with a piece of art, and Rudi left him with an invitation to dinner the next time Max was in town.

The rest of the day, Max emptied the crates. Wood shavings secured each piece of art. Hours later, Max took the last piece of art out—a Meissen figurine—placing it on the floor in front of him. Looking around him, he saw the room was a disaster. There were wood shavings on the floor everywhere. There, among the artwork, the cabinet stood proud in the corner. Max told Ernst Ritter he would send him the money when he sold the cabinet. Max was pleased with himself. The ordeal was over without a scratch on him. He did not want to think what would have happened to him if things had gone bad.

His mother told him to call Muller, the same antique dealer who was a close friend of hers and his father in Erfurt. Muller had moved to the West before East Germany closed their border in 1961. He owned a small gallery on the affluent main boulevard, Königsallee. Max knew he would appraise his art in Western currency, including US dollars.

Muller visited the apartment the next day. He not only told Max how much each piece was worth, he also told him he would help him sell his art.

"Don't go crazy, Max. You will never be able to get back the art that you sell."

For the next few days, Max was busy. He called the largest auction house in Düsseldorf and talked to Hans Schulman, his father's friend from Amsterdam. He lived in Düsseldorf now and had a gallery in the city. Also, Max had his mother send a letter to the museum in Nurembock. Max didn't want to leave the cabinet at his mother's apartment. It was too valuable. He wanted to know if they were interested in buying the cabinet for their museum.

Before he left to go home, he had sold $10,000 worth of art to the antique dealer, Hans Schulman, and to the local auction house. Max opened a bank account and deposited all the money he made from the sale of his art. He sold the Aphrodite head, a Roman copy from the second century, and other valuable antiquities, which he realized later was a big mistake.

At the same time, the curator from the Nurembock Museum made a special trip to see the cabinet after she had received his letter.

"Mr. Diesel, it is beautiful and so well-preserved," she said. "The museum would love to have the cabinet, but we do not have the funds to buy it now."

Max saw an opportunity to delay payment to Ernst Ritter. He had a potential buyer who was eager to make an offer. Max offered her a plan.

"The museum can have it as a loan while it raises the money to buy it," he said.

She was thrilled and thanked him repeatedly. He was relieved. Later on, he found out it was one of the museum's most important pieces of furniture on display.

Chapter 44

Max was excited to go home. After one week, he had ten thousand dollars in his pocket. He felt like a rich man. He gave his mother five thousand dollars for her help and to cover the inconvenience of leaving his art in the back room.

"I am so happy for you, Max. Look at all the money selling art can bring you." She smirked as she thought about the money.

"I'm coming back in one month to sell more."

Max could not get the thrill of dealing art out of his mind. He watched and learned from Hans Schulman. He sat next to Hans at one fine art auction and observed the sleight of hand and the importance of a face void of expression. But the hardest thing for Max to do was to sit through the silence. Max kept asking him questions, and Muller kept telling him to be quiet.

"Max, you must learn to talk with your eyes and hands, not your mouth."

"Impossible!" Max said.

Muller laughed. "Give it some time. You will get the hang of it." Muller encouraged Max because he had a good eye and a good feeling about art, just like his father. Max wanted to nurture that feeling, and the payback was a good incentive.

When he returned to his home in the States, he sought out small auctions and galleries in the city. His excitement grew when he bought at a good price, and he was getting used to the silence. He quickly developed a sober poker face.

He calculated his work time. His boss didn't care how he spent his days, as long as he produced and made money for the company. He couldn't wait to get back to Germany to buy and sell more art. He was unaware how obsessed he was becoming over his newfound passion.

It was the last days of May 1976. The long Memorial Day weekend gave him the time and excuse to fly to Germany. He was eager to attend one or two auctions in Düsseldorf. He was greeted by the smell of flowers in the warm air. Around the square, the colorful vendors claimed their space. Their open-air carts were filled with fresh produce and small items like jams and mustards, prepared foods like small ham-and-cheese sandwiches, and curry bratwurst sausage.

The aromas followed him along as he breathed it all in. He sprinted to the bank to withdraw some Western marks. He counted his money. He was in such a good mood until he asked for his balance. He discovered a large deposit had been made to his account—twenty-thousand dollars. His entire attitude shifted as his strong instincts triggered his curiosity. He rushed out of the bank, hailed a taxi, and went straight to his mother's house. He brushed a kiss across his mother's cheek as he hurried past her to the back room. He counted each piece of art and noticed there were pieces missing.

"I don't see the four hand-colored screens."

"Oh, a dealer from Spain was interested in the screens," Zelda said. "He gave an excellent price for them. I deposited the money—twenty thousand dollars—into your account. I thought you would be pleased."

Something was not right. Muller had appraised them for sixty thousand dollars. There were other pieces missing.

"Where are the other pieces? The military scenes in watercolor?"

"I sold them as well. I deserved to have some of the art. I should have taken more when I left for the West. After all, I was married to your father. The art should be mine also."

His face turned a bright red. He could feel all the pain from his youth rise to the surface in pent-up anger. Pacing back and forth, Max tried to control himself.

"I gave you money. You didn't have to steal from me. I would have given you more if you asked." A look of disdain for her covered his face. "When I sell some antiques, I am having the rest shipped to the United States."

The next day, he walked by the gallery of Hans Schulman. In the window were his screens. He went in to talk to Hans about his mother.

"Your mother sold me the screens for sixty thousand dollars," Hans said. "I had assumed you gave her permission."

"Thank you, Hans." Storming out of the shop, he realized she had not changed at all.

Once he had secured arrangements for the packing and shipment of his art to the United States, Max returned home. He was cool and distant with his mother, only speaking a few words to her before he left.

He waited all summer for his art to arrive by ship. They called him from customs to come and sign for his shipment. He hired movers to pick up the two huge crates to take to his house.

It took Max a few days to empty the crates. His house was overtaken by the artwork. He loved it. He couldn't get over the satisfaction his art gave him. He felt surprisingly complete.

He was engrossed in placing each piece in the right space, and he did not stop until everything was perfect.

For the first time, he understood his father's need for art and his obsession to have it in his possession. Nothing satisfied him so much as having his art around him.

He pictured all the art he had to leave behind in the East. Would he ever be able to get it back from the museums? He thought, *No chance of that happening.*

He was lucky to get as much as he did out of the East, and going back was not an option. He was no fool. The threats were real. He had to accept it and move on with his life.

He continued to sell his artifacts at auction in cities throughout the States. He gathered some pieces to take to Germany for interested buyers and planned to travel to Germany again after the holidays. Little did he realize he was buying more art for himself than he was selling. He was becoming an *art collector.*

Chapter 45

Meanwhile, in Erfurt, there was something about to happen that would change the course of events for Maximilian Diesel. The directors of the museums of Erfurt and Dresden went back to Emil's house to pick up the rest of the art they had tagged for their museums. They were like dogs with their tongues hanging out, waiting to devour a special treat.

They walked through the house, checking off their lists as they found each piece that had their mark on it. The Dresden director looked bewildered.

"Where is the German chinoiserie cabinet? I do not see it anywhere. It was not to go out of this house," he said.

Dr. Brewer cowered in the kitchen. His worst nightmare was about to happen. He was the one who let the cabinet go with Max.

With his head high, Brewer stood firm in front of the director. "I made the decision to let Mr. Diesel take it as part of his inheritance since it was appraised so low. I thought you had changed your mind, thinking it was not as important as you once thought it to be, and Mr. Diesel wanted it so much."

The Dresden director felt his fists tightened. He listened to Dr. Brewer and was trying to understand.

"You are blaming me? We all priced the inventory low. That was our strategy so we all could acquire more art since each piece was applied toward Mr. Diesel's tax bill. That cabinet was the most important piece of furniture Emil had in his collection. How could you let it go?"

Dr. Brewer tried to appear stunned and innocent. The Dresden director stormed out of the room.

None of them said another word. They gathered the rest of their art as fast as they could. The vans were loaded with their prized possessions. The house was emptied.

The next day, the Dresden director called the culture and finance department agents who were involved in the transfer. He lodged a formal complaint. The agents knew the cabinet was valuable and was supposed to remain in East Germany. They stammered over their apologies to the director. Unbeknownst to him, they had let the cabinet go because Ernst had rewarded them with gifts of art, money, and goods. In other words, they took the bribe.

The blame catapulted to the top. The customs agent got the Stasi involved. He came down on Dr. Brewer, the director of the Gera Museum, with a vengeance. Dr. Brewer squealed on Ernst Ritter, the state prosecutor and Stasi officer. Brewer told the Stasi that Ernst told him that he had gotten the approval from the finance and culture departments to let Mr. Diesel take 10 percent of his inheritance out of East Germany. Marlene was detained in Berlin as a knowing accomplice. The Dresden director proclaimed ignorance.

Dr. Brewer and Ernst Ritter were arrested for collusion. The finance and culture department agents got a slap on their hands and lost their jobs for receiving bribes from Ritter. Marlene was arrested, but she was released on probation. She was fortunate to have a husband in Berlin who was a high-ranking Stasi officer. Dr. Brewer and Ernst Ritter were imprisoned. The fact that Ritter was a Stasi officer couldn't even protect him under GDR Law. He was an example of what happens to rogue Stasi officers.

At the trial, Dr. Brewer and Ernst Ritter blamed their demise on one person—Maximilian Diesel. They each cried for mercy. "This capitalist from the West bribed us with art, money, and gifts. It was all his idea. It was Diesel's fault that the cabinet was taken out of the GDR, along with his inheritance."

The news of the trial circulated throughout the art circles of East Germany that summer. In the beginning of September, as the temperatures cooled and the leaves turned to gold, Marie was frightened for Max. The repercussions could be grave for him. She called him. She prayed he would be home.

Chapter 46

Max answered the telephone. Marie's voice cracked as she spoke his name. "Maximilian, I have news. It is not good."

"It's Mother, isn't it?" Max said.

"No, Mother is fine."

She blurted out the news. "Ernst Ritter and Dr. Brewer were arrested for helping you take the cabinet and your art out of East Germany. Others were prosecuted too. Marlene was detained and got probation. There was a big trial. Ernst and Dr. Brewer were sent to jail for collusion."

"Jail? Ritter and Brewer are in jail?"

"Rumor has it that Ernst hung himself in jail, and Brewer died in jail from unknown causes. Maximilian, they blamed you! They said you bribed them with art, money, and gifts."

"So they are both dead. How can I defend myself?"

"Maximilian, do not return to the East, to Erfurt, ever again. They will arrest you when you enter the East at the border."

Max could not believe what he was hearing. "It is not true! I was forced to give them what they wanted. I was coerced into agreeing to their scheme. I took only what was mine—my inheritance."

"I know, Maximilian. I believe you."

Max was scared, but he was more concerned about Marie. "I promise I will not go to the East. Will I ever see you again?"

"I do not know, Maximilian. They will be watching me."

Shaking, Max dropped the phone. The conversation with Marie caught him off guard. He was mortified and afraid. He was glad he was home alone. He wouldn't tell anyone about Marie's telephone call, especially his wife. He did not want to cause her to panic. He poured himself a double scotch and sat in his chair. After several doubles, he watched the news on TV and went to sleep.

For several days, he followed the international news. There was nothing about Maximilian Diesel. He couldn't understand it and didn't want to think about it. He kept to himself, constantly watching over his shoulders. He thought they would have come after him by now. Months went by. Nothing happened, and no one came. The New Year of 1977 came without incident. He let go of his slight paranoia and laughed it off as if it were a big joke. They couldn't implicate him without implicating themselves.

So life continued in a grandiose way for Max.

He left for Düsseldorf with art to sell in the spring of 1977. Hans Schulman became his mentor as he was becoming quite proficient in selling art. He loved to hear stories about his father from Hans. If Hans knew about Max's predicament in the East, he never asked Max about it. They built a strong relationship. Each time he left Germany, he took money out of his bank account and packed his suitcase with clothes, goodies, and art from Europe.

No one discussed Maximilian and East Germany—not his mother, not family, not even friends. Perhaps it was better not to know in case they were being watched.

Max appeared to have erased it from his mind.

Chapter 47

It was 1987. Ten years had passed. Max worked hard and smart at his day job. His marriage was the same. Their independent lifestyles agreed with them, and having a baby did not change it.

His passion for art grew. He had fallen in love with the world of art. His house became more like a museum than a home. Books were stacked ten high on the floor. Library bookcases overflowed with resource books about antiquities. In the beginning, his intention was to sell what he had bought at auction, but it never worked out that way. The pieces came home and never left the house again.

Max had brought the sought-after German chinoiserie cabinet to the States when the ten-year agreement ended. The museum in Nurembock was not happy to see it go, but he did not want to have any more aristocrats coming out of small German towns, claiming to own his cabinet.

In 1977, while the cabinet was in Nurembock, an aristocrat, heir to the family who owned the cabinet, sued Maximilian for the sole rights. He claimed Emil Diesel had bought lost art. It was lost during WWII, when his father hid it from the Russians. Maximilian told him he had documents from his father proving that it was a legitimate sale.

The aristocrat had waited for his father to die before he came forward to file the suit against Max. He read in the Nurembock newspaper about the new acquisition to the museum and realized it was the same cabinet that had been in his family for a long time.

Max was determined to fight for the cabinet, spending $200,000 to prove it was his. What clinched the case for Max was his witness, the baroness, wife of the owner. Under oath, she stated that her husband sold it to an art dealer in Nurembock, and she had the bill of sale with her. The dealer sold it to Muller's father, and Emil bought the cabinet from Muller's father, using money and art in trade.

The case went to two higher courts before the verdict fell in favor of Maximilian. He had written proof of the sale. Maximilian won the case and did not have to pay any money to the aristocrat who brought the suit against him. The aristocrat had to pay not only his attorney and court fees but Max's fees as well.

Max brought his cabinet home. Several years later, he almost sold it. At times, he was reckless with money from his small inheritance when cash got tight. He enjoyed the good life too much—fine wines, designer clothes, and new friends to party with.

It would have been a huge mistake to sell the cabinet. Thank goodness the museum that wanted to buy it backed out when they heard there had been a lawsuit over the ownership. It was a close call. He realized it would have been his greatest regret, and he would not have forgiven himself.

He regretted selling the Roman Aphrodite head and the other valuable objects from his father's collection. He was never able to get them back. Just like his father, Max's collection became the most important part of his life.

Chapter 48

On November 4, 1989, a million GDR citizens assembled in Alexanderplatz in the biggest demonstration in the history of their country. They demanded freedom of the press, freedom of assembly, and freedom of speech. These demands ushered in the democracy movement.

They were tired of the economic instability of the GDR, and there was talk among people about reunification with the West. Erich Honecker, leader of the GDR and the party, had resigned on October 18, 1989. His successor, Egon Krenz, could not contain the people.

On November 9, 1989, at a press conference, a member of the Politburo (the SED cabinet) announced the lifting of visa requirements necessary to leave the GDR. Word spread fast in the GDR, and the news in the West picked it up, announcing, "GDR opens its borders." People shouted, "Let us out!" Thousands of East Berliners ran to the inner-city checkpoints. The barriers were raised shortly after midnight. The checkpoints were open.

The wall fell *that night*.

Max listened to news broadcasts repeating the historic events all week. His head ached as bitter memories flooded his mind. He realized he was free to travel to East Germany, which meant he could return to Erfurt. He had put the whole awful episode in Erfurt behind him, burying it way back in his mind. It was as if it never happened, and he was determined to keep it that way. He could not go back to the East again. He was terrified of *what* or *who* was waiting for him there.

He did not return to Germany until after the reunification of the GDR and the federal republic on October 3, 1990. The two Germanys and the four allies from WWII formed the Two Plus Four Agreement in February 1990, safeguarding the political future of Berlin. It set the course for a free and united Germany. Moscow finally relinquished their rights all over Germany, and within four years, they withdrew all their occupying troops.

Max flew back to Düsseldorf several times to buy and sell art, often staying with his mother. But there was no mother-and-son bond.

Even now, he was blind not to see that he was still trying to get her love and attention. Their relationship remained guarded because of her jealousy and his mistrust. As long as the past was never mentioned, they could converse with little tension. His mother enjoyed listening to Max talk about his travels around the world. She talked about the new unified Germany and celebrities in the news and gossiped about her friends and their indiscretions.

When she expressed her resentment toward him, the past crept into the present.

"You have a good job and life, and you don't work too hard. Everything always comes easy to you. Look what I have—nothing— and I am ailing and in pain all over."

At first, Max felt guilty and tried to help her, but it was never good enough. She was a great actor. The next time, she laid the guilt on thicker. Max didn't fall for it all. He played along, seeing right through the deceit.

"Yes, I don't call often and come to see you enough. It is my fault. I am so busy these days." The truth was, he never felt like talking to her on the phone because all she would do was complain about her ailments and him. He became indifferent to her drama.

"I have to go now," he would say to her. "I have work to do." His impatience grew with every word he uttered.

One time, Max sent her a ticket to come and visit them in the States. It was 1989. He took her sightseeing, and she spent time with the family. She had little tolerance for children, even Max and Helga's little daughter, her granddaughter. It wasn't long before she told Max not to bring his daughter over to Germany until she was old enough to go for lunch and carry on a conversation.

Max was determined to be a better father and husband than his father, it didn't turn out that way. It was evident by his flamboyant lifestyle that his parents weren't the best role models while he was growing up. When he wasn't working, he was gallivanting with his artistic friends—a grim reminder of his father.

He and his wife stopped making an effort to spend time together. She would go to bed early, and he would go to bed late. They each took turns being mother and father because of their jobs. Their daughter grew up strong-willed and independent, just like them. Max and his wife grew apart. It was no surprise to either of them. A mutual separation and cordial divorce followed.

Chapter 49

Max had become a true collector when he met Sophie in the late nineties. She was American. His weekly visits to auctions became the norm. He craved the hunt for the best deal. He had such a vast knowledge of art; he felt he could compete with any curator at any museum. He was proud of himself and his art collection, just like his father.

He introduced Sophie to his world of art. A day in the city was not complete if it did not include a visit to a museum or gallery or auction. A little shopping was added for her pleasure, and a lavish dinner with the best wine followed. Along with the fine ambiance, Max expected excellence, which he always got. Sophie got caught up in this whirlwind romance within a short time.

Each day Sophie spent with Max, she experienced more of his sophisticated personality and his flair for drama. She listened to his stories, like a young child listening to her teacher reading fairy tales from a book. Enamored by his engaging personality, she fell for him hard. He did not let go of his late-night shenanigans with his friends at the clubs in town. He liked his independence too much, which was difficult for Sophie.

Sophie was warm, patient, quiet, and sensitive. She was also strong-minded and idealistic, and she had an impulse for adventure. She had long wavy chestnut hair and big brown eyes. She wanted his attention too.

"This relationship is not going to work, Max. We are different. We are polar opposites."

"I thought that was supposed to be a good thing," he said.

She tried to end the relationship, but he was persistent. He showed her that he wanted to be with her, giving up the late nights with the boys. He convinced her they were perfect for each other, and at last she agreed. He always made her laugh and smile even after their most heated discussions.

They married soon after.

They spent the next several years traveling the world, learning as much about each other as the exotic and romantic places they visited.

When they settled down at home, she overlooked his emotional outbursts and his commanding, loud voice when things did not go his way.

"It's not important to get yourself so upset. Nothing is perfect," she would say calmly.

"You're right. It's never been easy for me to accept that perfection does not exist, especially when I see it in my art every day."

A heartfelt apology was followed with a joke and a big grin. Of course, Sophie always accepted his apology.

This was how life was for Max and Sophie—an ebb and flow, like rivers flowing into the sea.

Part IV

Resolution
2010–Present

Chapter 50

It was spring of 2012. Two years had passed since the last meeting in Germany. The tulips had come and gone, and winter jackets had been stored away in the cedar closet. Flower boxes were filled with bright-yellow pansies, purple petunias, and white geraniums, and the deck had become part of the house again.

Sophie and Max were still waiting—and believing.

From this unjust era, there was *hope* for *justice* rousing within this time capsule they were thrust into. They bore witness to moments of happiness and pain, torment and anguish, beauty and obsession. Despite those tumultuous times, Emil triumphed in building a grand art collection. His legacy, along with his death, would be acknowledged and avenged. They could feel it. They could taste it.

The opening of the time capsule would be sweet and bountiful for Max, Sophie, and Emil.

The Himalayan mask did not seem as frightening these days for Max. That mask had provoked him to confront his past with conviction. He faced it all with certainty that he would prevail because truth was on his side.

Today, the telephone call to Max from the attorney was optimistic.

Max shouted to Sophie from the sitting room, "Get the champagne from the wine cooler. I have good news from Becker! We will meet with the judges and finance department soon."

Sophie did not jump up and down this time. She pulled her jeans up around her hips and slipped a soft, colorful, green-and-blue-striped

T-shirt over her head. She slid into her blue suede flats, brushed her long chestnut hair, and sauntered downstairs through the winding hallway, through the kitchen, and into the sitting room.

Like Max, as she walked, her eyes followed each painting and drawing that hung on the walls. Sophie had grown very fond of the art around her. She had developed an intimate bond with the paintings, the sculpture, and porcelain, especially with the Buddhas that blessed the living room, their bedroom, and the dining room. The wooden saint that stood across from the entrance of their bedroom made her feel safe. Falling asleep was easy because he was there.

Occasionally, she would say to Max, "He is watching you, so you better be good."

As she entered the sitting room, she passed by the carved wooden statue of a saintly woman embracing a young girl. It sat on top of the French marble table. Two cherub angels that graced a mirror above the statue always reminded her of her mom. She felt love all around her.

She did not rush to get the champagne. She turned to Max, making that look with her deep-brown eyes that raised her eyebrows.

"Max, when will we meet them?" She was skeptical because she had heard this news so many times before.

"Soon, soon. It could be as early as November."

She knew that it could be January, February, March, even April, because once the holidays came, all of Germany would be on an extended holiday.

Sophie had let go of any expectations so there would be no disappointments. She thought it made life so much easier to deal with when you have no expectations.

They seemed happy and satisfied with each other; an air of contentment had filled their New England home. Their best moments were spent together alone, watching television or reading a book. Max would extend his hand to her, and she would reach out to grasp it. He would hold her hand as if it were a cherished antique vessel.

With a satisfied smile, he would blow kisses and confess, "I have never been so happy with anyone. I do love you, Sophie. Don't ever doubt my love for you."

Sophie would smile back. "Never."

Still there was not a day that went by that each one did not think about Germany. His home office was strewn with his files and documents about the case. He knew what each document was and where it was, and these documents could not be disturbed by anyone (that meant Sophie, even though the mess drove her wild).

Newspaper clippings were scattered about the documents from all the major newspapers in Germany—*Die Tag* (Hamburg), *Die Abendnachrichten* (Berlin), and including the scandalous paper *Der Informant* (Hamburg). They each told the story of Max's fight for his inheritance and had photos of him and his father. The story was still alive in Germany.

Sophie looked around her. Her eyes had fallen upon the Renoir-style statue of a beautiful young woman's curvaceous body. His art had become her life too.

When would justice be served to them? She knew it was not fair for the museums to hold on to his art, but life was not fair. They had to fight for their rights.

Chapter 51

In Erfurt, a subtle change had been made at the Gera Museum. Marie noticed the article in the newspaper. She was quick to inform Max about the change. His cell phone's "old telephone" ringtone alerted him to the call.

"Marie, how are you?" A huge grin stretched across his face. "What's happening over there?"

"Max, you are not going to believe it. I read a small article in the newspaper today regarding Dr. Morgan, the director of the Gera Museum. He was replaced. Dr. Ludwig from the former East Germany is the new director. The article stated that Dr. Morgan took another position as a curator in the same museum and now answers to this new director, his new boss. The new museum director now answers to the head of the culture department. I have an idea he was pushed out of his position by Mrs. Mitzer, who is still the official in charge of culture."

"Marie, you could be right. It is interesting that he was replaced at the same time our case is pending in court for review. I am sure the newspapers had something to say about the change. They know that Mrs. Mitzer, a Left Party member from the former East Germany, oversees the museums in Erfurt. She can't be trusted."

For one nervous moment, Max relapsed into a frightening thought. *Maybe someone is listening. I better be careful about what I say on the phone.*

Was this paranoia the result of his life in Germany?

He composed himself. "Sorry, Marie. Let me continue," Max said. "It does make sense that Dr. Ludwig would replace Dr. Morgan, who was from the West, with someone who thinks the same way as she does and at least knows how to play along. No doubt, Dr. Morgan did not agree with her political and cultural views pertaining to the Gera Museum. I remember he was sympathetic toward us when we attended the meeting at the museum in 2006. He remarked how difficult it was for him to deal with former East German staff members of the museum. Then I thought his silence was strange when we went back to fight our case in 2010. He appeared to be against us."

It was interesting that no one mentioned that Dr. Morgan had been picked up by Mrs. Mitzer's security guards on his way to work the week before his position changed at the Gera Museum. Forced into a shiny white van, he was blindfolded and taken to a small vacant warehouse on the outskirts of the city.

Shaken, Dr. Morgan was asked to sit at the long rectangular metal table in the middle of the room. He heard the sound of heavy, loud steps approaching him. His blindfold was slowly removed, causing his eyes to blink and squint wildly. A large muscular figure stood before him.

"Dr. Morgan, don't be alarmed. I just want to ask you a few questions regarding Maximilian Diesel. Would you like a glass of water?"

"Yes, please." He was quite confused by the unfolding drama.

"Do you have any information we could use against Mr. Diesel's case? Where did he get his inventory? We heard you gave it to him. How well do you know Mr. Diesel? We do not want this case to be heard in court."

He remained calm and fixed to the chair. "I don't have any information other than him wanting his father's art back that was taken by the East Germans. I didn't give him anything. He had documents in his hands already. He appears to be determined to get back what is rightfully his, and I agreed with him. The Stasi took the art, and he should have all of it returned to him. Even if it means a great loss to the museum."

"Our case with the finance department is coming up soon, whether we settle or go to court again," Max said. "She is aware of this, so we will have to see how she will use Dr. Ludwig to her advantage. And I doubt the new director knows about our case. I wonder if when we do face her, she will bring Dr. Morgan into the meeting since he was involved early on and understands our case so well. Thanks for calling, Marie. It seems we will see you soon."

"You must come and spend a few days in Burg with me and Horst."

"Sounds great. I do hope it will be soon. Our attorney is supposed to call in September with the date for the meeting. I will let you know when I know."

Max pressed *end* and shoved the phone back in his pocket. He was also getting tired of waiting. This time, he didn't want to show his disappointment in front of Sophie. He saw how frustrated she was about the waiting game Erfurt was playing. He had to have the positive attitude and keep the fight alive.

Keeping the faith for Max was not easy to do. From childhood he had not relied on faith. Faith was not a topic of discussion. He had learned from his mother and father that trust in anything or anyone was elusive—no wonder he had difficulty trusting others.

He had been taught to believe in himself to make life happen and to be responsible for his own actions. Despite his dysfunctional family life, he was grateful his parents and grandparents were all strong, independent thinkers. They were survivors who taught him right and wrong and ingrained in him the moral and legal obligation to be accountable for himself.

Max walked with determination into the living room with his whiskey glass in his hand. Lights were dimmed. Mozart's symphony filled the room. He sat in the corner of the sofa and gazed at the mantel, where several objects sat. A painted porcelain head of a cat, a Japanese ivory carved box, and the golden-bronze Buddha captured his attention. The eighteenth-century mirror tilted just enough to show off an impressive gilded baroque-style frame.

"This is perfect," he muttered. "Life is good."

Closing his eyes, he let the music fill his head, drifting off to dreams of another time. His father was holding his small hand as they wandered through the museum. He was tired and told his father he wanted to rest. He could feel his father's grip tighten around his hand.

"Max, I want none of that talk," he said. "You must forget yourself and focus only on what you see around you. Lose yourself in the art, become the people in the painting, and you will not feel tired but excited. Max, the past, present, and future are in front of you. If you do not see it now, you will with time."

In the dimly lit room, he rubbed his teary eyes and looked up as if hoping to see his papi standing in front of him.

He did not understand it then.

Now he understood it. It was so clear.

Max knew he could not live without his possessions around him. Through each object, he could feel the connection with his past and with his father. Art grounded him in the present. It gave him purpose.

Max realized, *We are just caretakers of art passing through time. Art survives. That is all that matters. Each piece tells our history. It is our gift to future generations. It is our legacy.* Only art could have told his father's story about the man he was.

Max discovered his love of art was universal. His preoccupation with artifacts, and so many like him, could be controlled. He understood his father's obsessive connection with his art. Only Emil had let it rule his life. It radiated through him like energy from the sun. It came first as a passion then as an addiction. Max realized the potential danger of obsessing over art. Like a drug, it could cost him the loss of his family, money, time, and even his life.

Here was a true Greek tragedy. "Look!" he shouted for all to hear. "It cost my father his life!" Emil was the protagonist; his life quest for art, his conflict. His struggle with his family, who desperately needed him, was against a stronger, more powerful force—his destiny to be a great collector. Only it was all ripped away from him, thus ending tragically with his death.

Max raised his glass to his father. "To you, Papi. It will not be for nothing." He swallowed his drink until it was gone. That night, Max made a resolution—a silent resolution—filled with love and happiness.

He was never to allow art to consume him like it did his father. Max had too much love and respect for family, friends, and life to lose it all to art.

More determined than ever to restore his father's legacy, he had to win his case and retrieve his father's art, his inheritance. He had no intention of wasting time thinking about what he would do with the collection when he got it. He would figure that out later.

Hands by his side, he hoisted himself from the sofa to look for Sophie. It did not stop him from pausing and turning his head to glance at the white-seated Buddha on the French marble table. He called out to her and walked toward the hallway. He needed her now. He depended on her to lift his spirits. He needed to see her smile and to laugh at her frustrated efforts to dodge his playful hands.

His gaze met hers. He held her close and kissed her lips, taking her breath away.

"Wow, what was that for?"

"I missed you. That is all."

She ran her fingers through his hair to rearrange the fine white strands and whispered, "Still a good-looking man. Napping again, I see."

"I do enjoy it. I am ready to go," he commanded as he took her by the hand.

"Really?" She didn't believe him.

"Let's go out for dinner tonight. Come. I need to get out of the house."

She agreed. "I'll get my jacket. I am ready to go!"

Chapter 52

Sophie sat sideways on the bar stool to make sure Max's attention was on her. She wanted to hear what Marie had told him earlier. He loved sitting at the bar when it was just the two of them. He would mingle with strangers who might sit next to him and banter with the bartenders. If she did not get his attention first, she knew she would have a difficult time getting it back.

Max sipped his martini with delight. He liked the vodka stirred, not shaken, no ice, with a spray of vermouth, and with olives on the side. The tiny bubbles of her chilled champagne tickled her palate as she sipped from the crystal flute.

"Mmmm . . . lightly fruity, and not too dry." She was totally enjoying the experience.

"Sophie!" Max shouted to get her attention. "Dr. Morgan was replaced by a new director at the Gera Museum. I don't think it will cause a problem for our case. We have all the documents to back us up even if he is not at the next meeting. Our case is in the judge's hand. Don't worry, okay?"

Sophie sighed and took another sip. "I know we will win our case. I am not worried about that. It's the waiting that's making me doubt that it will happen at all." She placed her empty glass on the bar, thinking about what might lie ahead for them.

After a fine dinner and a pleasant conversation with the owner, Sophie drove home. Max reclined his seat and closed his eyes while they enjoyed the classical music station. She cherished the drive in complete silence. On this dark, clear night, the full moon lit the way home.

She thought this summer was one of the best summers they had enjoyed at home in a long time. On warm, sunny days, they had lounged on the deck, surrounded by plush green lawns and lush flower gardens. And on starry nights, they enjoyed outdoor grilling with friends and dreaming about their future.

The rest of the summer was more of the same. Fall was not far off, and Dr. Becker would be calling in September to give them the date of the next important meeting. They stayed close to home, not venturing into the city often, not even visiting the museum where their precious piece was on display.

Stretched out on the sofa, his head on Sophie's lap, Max said, "We haven't been to the museum all summer. I wonder if our cabinet is still there. The museum was excited to acquire such a valuable and important piece of European furniture. I know it's in the right place, although there are times when I have second thoughts about loaning it to them."

Sophie laughed. "I am sure it's still there. Let's go soon."

"I would like that a lot." His thoughts wandered back to the past and what he had to do to claim his cherished piece. It was a bittersweet experience—pride and joy coupled with regret.

Summer seemed to pass into fall without fanfare. When they did not hear from Dr. Becker, it was very clear they would not be going to Germany for the meeting until the spring. After the holidays, they reveled in the quiet months of winter. They would curl up in front of the fireplace with a book in hand. On the coldest days, everything seemed to slow down, as if to catch a breath and a yawn from a deep sleep.

Another year had passed. It was a sunny February morning in 2013. Sophie snuggled into the pillows of the sofa as she read the morning newspaper. She was engrossed in the editorial when Max teased her by waving a letter-size sheet of paper in front of her face. Finally, he gave in and let her look at the German letterhead. It had an impressive seal stamped on it in the shape of a German shield or a coat of arms.

Across the header was printed in bold letters Thuringer Finanzgericht (Thuringer Finance Court).

"Max, read it to me, please. "

"It says, 'To Maximilian Diesel, regarding the case of Emil Diesel from 1965 to 1975, there will be a court hearing the second quarter of this year.' That is April, May, or June."

Sophie two-stepped around the coffee table and jumped into Max's arms. She wrapped her arms around his neck. "Max, I can't believe it. At last we are going to Germany. It will be over soon. You will have your inheritance!"

"Don't get too excited. We still have the finance court hearing to endure. Then we can celebrate."

She stepped back and caught her breath. "I know. I am excited. It feels like we have been waiting forever."

He laughed at her. "Start packing your bags. You know how long it takes you, even if it is only two bags."

Sophie smiled coyly and ran to get her travel book. She flipped to the page where the trip to Northern Italy was tagged.

"You promised we would go to Italy after we finished our business in Germany."

"Let's talk about it later." He saw that smile change to a slight frown.

One day, they looked around them and realized spring was rolling in with delicate rain that woke up the crocuses and daffodils. Remnants of snow lingered around the bushes and grass. Max contemplated his gardens as he looked out from the deck. Some daisies had to be replaced, and the delphiniums needed to be moved to the back. Sophie calculated time for spring cleaning. Closets needed to be thinned out, and old magazines piled high had to be sorted—some to go and some to keep.

Despite their busy days, in the back of their minds, they were anticipating the call from Germany. They knew it would be soon. They were eager to go.

May and June slid by. The beauty and fragrance of July flowers and herbs filled the garden landscape, and the flower boxes lining the deck were in full bloom.

It was a sign. Their case was delayed again. Frustrated, they decided not to dwell on it anymore. They went about enjoying the balmy summer days.

One early morning, Max looked down at the text message left on his phone: "I will call you at 10:00 a.m., your time, Dr. Karl Becker."

"Finally," he whispered to himself. He stared at the phone and stroked it like a fine piece of porcelain, wondering about the conversation he would soon have with his attorney.

He placed his phone on the night table beside his bed and turned over toward Sophie. She had not moved at all. She lay on her side, one leg straight and the other bent over a pillow that lay underneath it. Chuckling, he could not believe she slept through all the commotion.

He brought his face close to hers and, in a faint loud voice, said, "Sophie, wake up. Dr. Becker is calling soon."

She tried to open her sleepy eyes, but they were not cooperating. They were heavy, filled with dreams pulling her away from consciousness. "Huh, Max, I'm still sleeping." Her mind and body succumbed again to her dreams. He knew he was not going to get any response or encouragement until she woke up. He flipped himself over and hoisted himself out of bed.

An hour and a half later, Sophie shuffled her feet down the stairs, through the hallways, and into the kitchen. She poured a large cup of steaming black coffee and eased herself into her chair.

Max smiled. "Awake at last!"

She returned the smile with a laugh. "I'm sorry, Max, but you know my beauty sleep is very important to me."

"Dr. Becker will call this morning at ten, Sophie. Pack your bags. I do believe we are taking a trip to Germany."

Dr. Becker returned his call, precisely at ten. German punctuality—Max loved it. They spoke only for a brief time. Sophie watched his head nod each time as he said, "Yah, yah."

After placing his phone back on the counter, he turned to hug Sophie.

"The court hearing is on December 5 in Lothe, a small town near Erfurt. Becker will e-mail all the information regarding the case, including time and place. We will meet him the day before in Erfurt to go over the case, and we will go together to the finance court. There will be three judges and two volunteer judges, also the plaintiff, the finance department head, the defense, and attorneys. Representatives from the museums will be there as well."

His voice was loud and trembling. "This is going to be big, Sophie! Becker did not notify the press. He wants to keep it quiet for now. They all want to keep it quiet. Make all the reservations when he sends us the itinerary."

"Okay." She returned a small hand salute. Sophie could feel the hairs stand up on her arms. She thought, *Is this excitement or nerves?*

The summer and fall were a blur. Then the time came fast.

Deep in thought, she packed her bags in silence. She remembered the first time they went to Germany. She packed for business this time. Her light-green wool skirt and deep-violet wool boxy top would do just fine. She reached for her jeans and blue swing sweater. She repacked Max's bag, adding two striped shirts, an extra pair of gray pants, and brown shoes, thinking there was always room for pleasure. Perhaps she could persuade Max to take a short side trip to Switzerland or Belgium. Feeling a huge grin spread across her face, she folded with extra care one gorgeous dress for a special evening.

Chapter 53

December wasn't their favorite time to visit Germany. Frankfurt Airport terminals were as busy as ever. The holidays were coming. People were running to grab the shuttles to catch the long-distance trains. They were among them, lugging their luggage up and down the escalators. Because of bad weather to the north, they had to take the longer commuter train, stopping at each town along the way. It was the safer route. Max took a snooze. Sophie stared out the window. Foggy gray skies and wet pavements changed to snow-covered fields to dry, barren ground. Trees, naked without their leaves, stood tall like guardians of the valleys surrounding the towns. Horses with thick coats grazed among them. It was 1600 hours (5:00 p.m.) when the train pulled into Erfurt.

It was a bitter, cold day. Dusk was falling around them. Their pace quickened. Sophie wrapped her scarf around her neck twice to secure her fur-lined hood, which would slip from her head as she walked gingerly on the cobblestone streets. Turning the corner, she could see the hotel. With her large tote slung over her shoulder, she pulled her wheeled bag beside her, hurrying into the hotel, huffing and puffing. They checked in at the desk. The hotel was the same. Nothing seemed to have changed except the weather.

They unpacked and decided to go to the fair for dinner. The Christmas fairs brought many of the local people out during the day. Each town or city took great pride in having the best fair around. Handmade goods like linens and jewelry were sold. All kinds of sausage—German, Polish, Hungarian—were prepared outdoors over open grills. Every type of food you could want, from cheese to chocolate, was sold. People ate under superlarge tents heated by open fire pits, many of them rubbing their hands together over the pits to warm their hands and body. Pale faces with ruddy cheeks peeked through hats and scarves. Fur-lined boots covered the manicured toes of the women. They decided on German sausage in a crisp roll with sauerkraut and onion, topped off with spicy mustard. They splashed it down with cold German beer. Satisfied, they sauntered back to the hotel. Max took a scotch upstairs. Sophie followed behind with hot chamomile tea. They flopped into bed, too tired to talk about the next day's meeting with Dr. Becker.

They woke early.

Sophie looked out the window. "Not a cloud in the sky. Let's get dressed."

They decided to have breakfast out. They strolled through the empty streets of Erfurt. Sophie tugged her warm shearling coat close to her body, tightened her scarf, and threw the hood around her head. With gloved hands in her pockets, the brisk morning chill made her walk a little faster, whereas Max walked easily with just a light quilted cashmere vest over a cashmere sweater against his chest. His wool hat and leather gloves were tucked in his pockets.

"Sophie, you are kidding. It's not cold at all."

"Max, I don't go by your thermostat. You're always warm." Anticipation overtook her. She took a cool, deep breath. "It is wonderful to be here again. Let's stop for coffee at that corner café."

"Sounds good to me." He opened the door for her. She rushed into the cozy room, relieved to be inside.

Neither of them heard the footsteps following behind them. They were too busy chatting with each other. Max followed behind her, smelling the brewing coffee and the sweet pastries. They sat at a small table by the wall that looked out into the room. Max could see everybody come and go. He liked it that way.

He did not notice the slender young man in a gray trench coat walk through the door behind them. He grabbed the morning newspaper, glancing up at them as if to get their attention then sitting down two tables in front of them. Max thought that was odd. Did he know them? Max dismissed his thoughts. He took a hearty sip of his dark, bold-tasting coffee, smacked his lips, and finished the last bite of his fruit-filled pastry.

Startled, he looked up and stared right into the face of the grinning man hovering over the table.

"Hello," the man said as if he was talking to an old friend. "I am a reporter from the local newspaper. I heard you were in town, Mr. Diesel, and I wanted to talk to you about the upcoming meeting. I wanted to know what your thoughts are regarding your case."

Max was more than irritated at the public display of rudeness. "What audacity you have to follow me, thinking that I would offer any opinions or thoughts I have about my case with you. Do you think I am stupid? You better leave now so I can pretend you were never here."

Deflated but not defeated, the young man frowned and walked away with his head down. He would try again another time. He was assigned to this story and had to figure out another way to interview Max before the meeting.

"Max, you were a little hard on him. He was just doing his job. He is the one who will write the way he sees you. You may need him."

"Sophie, the press is not supposed to know we are here. I wonder how it leaked out. We have to keep our guard up. We don't want to say anything to jeopardize our case. We are too close to getting our art back. The city tried to stall us with all the so-called legal procedures before going to finance court. It's time. It would be foolish for them to prolong the inevitable. We are getting our art back in the end."

"Max, it's getting so complicated."

"This is why tomorrow's hearing is so important. We must show them our determination to settle our case. It's in the best interest for all of us."

Weary from the constant confusion, Sophie shrugged her shoulders, got up from the table, and threw her coat on.

"Let's go. I need to walk." He grabbed her hand.

"It is going to be all right, Max. Patience."

They were aware while walking back to the hotel and realized that Erfurt had changed a little. New clothing stores with current trends and a variety of food vendors filled the square. Stray tourists who ventured off on their own mingled with the locals, who went about their daily business. Despite the change, Erfurt's quaint medieval surroundings were not disturbed. The Gera Museum's modern facade stood out from the trolley-lined streets, unaware that a dark secret had hung over the museum, which was about to be exposed.

Dr. Becker was to meet them at 1300 hours (1:00 p.m.) for lunch. He wanted to go over his remarks with them before the meeting. They went to their room to change, preoccupied by their own thoughts to notice each other's concern. Sophie sat quietly on the small sofa; tears welled up in her eyes. She could not stop them from finding their way down her cheeks.

Max saw her tremble and placed his hand on her shoulder. "It will be over soon. We will settle. Nothing will go wrong, Sophie. I promise."

Sophie took a deep calming breath. She wanted to believe Max. "It has been so long, Max. I just want it over."

"We have to meet Dr. Becker now. Why don't you put on your red knit dress? All eyes will be on you when you walk into the room."

Dr. Becker stood up smiling when he saw them. He greeted Max with a hearty handshake and a pat on the back. He hugged Sophie and commented on how stunning she looked. It had been almost four years since they had last seen one another. Dr. Becker looked the same, maybe a little thinner and a little gray at the temples. Sophie thought his wonderful smile was infectious. She returned a warm smile and a sigh in return.

After exchanging amenities, they settled down to the business at hand.

"This is it," Dr. Becker said. "This hearing will determine whether both sides can agree to settle this case. Each judge has read the case. They will state their findings and come to a conclusion regarding the parties involved. Each side will present their side of the case. The judges will deliberate after they hear each side.

"I am still confident that the judges will persuade everyone to settle. Going to a higher court would not be in their best interest. I think that they will not want this case to tie up the court, considering the amount of paperwork it will generate.

"They know we want the art instead of money, and we tried to settle with the museums. Since this is finance court, we may receive some money as compensation. Once we agree to settle, the cultural department and the museums have to comply. We will go over the inventory together and decide the art we want to take and the art we want to give to the museums. This will not take long.

"If this goes as smoothly as I just outlined, we will have won our case. Justice will be served for you and for your father. Of course, the judges could rule against us and agree with the defense—the finance department. Then we will have to endure another fight in court."

A shaken Max spoke. "That is the key word—*smoothly*. So far, nothing has gone smoothly. The finance department has been in constant disagreement with us."

Sophie was pleased Dr. Becker spoke in English. He thought it was important for her to hear what was going to happen because the hearing would be conducted in German. In a way, she was glad she did not understand the language. She didn't know if she could handle her emotions. She didn't want to make Max or Dr. Becker nervous during the proceedings.

"The hearing will begin at 9:15 a.m.," Dr. Becker said. "We will go together in a taxi to the courthouse in Lothe. Call me if you have any questions.

"Let's meet tonight for dinner at 1800 hours [6:00 p.m.] in the hotel's restaurant across from the patio. I will make sure they give us a quiet table in the corner. Max, I want to go over what you will say when the defense asks you questions. I want you to be ready for anything they might ask you."

"Thank you for everything you have done for us, Dr. Becker."

They had a good feeling they would win the case, even though their attorney alarmed them when he expressed his feelings of uncertainty.

They walked upstairs to their room without talking. It was overwhelming for both of them.

Sophie reached out and grabbed Max's hand. "What are you thinking, Max?"

"I don't know, Sophie. All this time, Dr. Becker has been so sure of himself, so confident that the outcome would be in our favor. Then at lunch, he wasn't so sure. His comments broke my confidence a little. I want to lie down for a while."

"Sounds wonderful. I'll join you." She hung her dress in the closet and removed her contacts. She pulled the covers over her, snuggled close to him, and closed her eyes, trying to forget for a moment where she was and why she was there. They both fell sound asleep.

Max awoke and quickly glanced at his watch. "Sophie, we have to get dressed and meet Dr. Becker. I don't want to be late. I will meet you at the restaurant. Don't be too long."

"I'll be right behind you, Max. I promise."

Max waved to Sophie from the back corner of the dining room. Her black wool pencil skirt clung around her hips as she moved toward the table. Her long-sleeved gold cashmere sweater shimmered and drew attention to her shoulder-length chestnut hair. She was beautiful to watch as her red mouth opened to greet him and the attorney.

Dr. Becker stood up and gently took both her hands in his. "You look lovely."

"Thank you." She looked around. "This is a great table." She lowered herself into her chair. She kissed Max on the lips and smiled. "Thank you for waiting for me."

"Dr. Becker," Max said, "I have got to ask you something. It has been bothering me for a while. We have gotten to know each other fairly well. I would like us to address each other by our first names. I feel it's appropriate now."

"Well, Mr. Diesel, that would be fine. We must toast on it. That is the tradition." He pushed his glasses up his nose. His blue eyes sparkled with delight.

"Wonderful. We consider you a friend."

"Max, you may not feel this way if we lose the case. When I last spoke to Dr. Krimpton, the head of the finance department, he was cocky and almost intimidating. He had said, 'Dr. Becker, your chance of winning your case against us is very slim. We win ninety-five percent of all the cases that come before us. My brilliant attorney has never lost a case."

A big grin appeared on Max's face, followed by a hearty laugh. "Karl, I'm not worried. We know we will win. Tomorrow we will be drinking champagne to celebrate."

They ordered champagne, clicking their glasses to solidify their friendship. They ordered a fine bottle of French red wine, which complemented their German dinners, and talked about their families before settling down to business.

Karl discussed with Max the answers to possible questions that could be posed by the judges and the finance department attorney. He went over his own remarks regarding the case with them and how he would present himself to the court.

"Max, we have all the evidence to win the case. I am prepared to do my job. Don't worry. One more day."

Max was worried. He was about to face his past.

Chapter 54

Sophie felt Max tossing in bed all night. The bed covers were scattered and thrown to her side of the bed. She squirmed out from under them and tossed her long hair back and forth, shaking it from her neck and shoulders. She stretched her arms out and felt the cool morning sunshine like crystals through the window.

"Wake up, Max. It's a beautiful morning. It's a sign."

Max stretched out his body, slowly unwrapping his arms from around his head that had cramped up as he unraveled them.

He rolled his eyes. "Sophie, what nonsense is a sign? I know the court will go our way. Our case is solid, and we all can walk away with something. We must be positive."

She flung her arms around his shoulders. "I love you, Max Diesel." She gave him a hard, luscious kiss and flung him back onto the bed. She moved close to him and felt how aroused he was. She moved on top of him and, with delight, finished what he started. He could not have been more pleased with his beautiful wake-up call.

"Sophie, it's time. We have to get dressed. We are meeting Karl for breakfast at 8:45 a.m. Let's meet again like this later. It will be my turn to please you."

Within minutes, Max was dressed in dark-blue pants, pale-peach shirt, gray sports jacket, and a blue-print tie. He had to look like he meant business.

"Sounds great. I'll hurry and be ready in fifteen minutes. I'll meet you downstairs."

He scowled. "Don't be late, Sophie."

Pouting, she rushed past him without saying a word, slamming the bathroom door behind her.

Max stared at his watch, counting down the minutes. He looked up to see Sophie standing in front of him. She looked so amazing in a green silk-and-wool skirt, white cashmere sweater, and black boots. She finished with diamond stud earrings and a diamond tennis bracelet.

"Two minutes to spare. Good job." He proudly kissed her on the lips.

"You have little faith, Max. Where's Dr. Becker?"

"He should be down in a few minutes. He had a phone call to make. Sit down, Sophie. I'll pour you coffee. Have something at the buffet if you want."

She rubbed her tummy. "I'm too nervous to eat. Maybe a little toast to satisfy my stomach."

"I couldn't eat either."

Max stood up and waved Dr. Becker to the table. Karl could barely hold his briefcase in one hand, his coat and scarf dangling over his arm, while juggling his books in the other hand. Another bag, which carried his robe for court, hung from his shoulder. His eyeglasses slipped down his nose. Using one finger, he pushed them up over his eyes. He looked like an absentminded professor, but they knew he was a methodical and resolute lawyer.

He looked up at them, rattled by his tardiness. "Sorry. I hope you started without me."

"We did, Karl. You should grab some breakfast. I'll have a fresh pot of coffee sent over to the table."

Becker left his gear and headed for the buffet.

After taking the last bite of his sweet toast covered with raspberry jam and sipping the last drop of coffee, he looked straight into their eyes. "Are you ready?"

"As ready as we will ever be," Max said.

"Then let's go and *win this case!*"

They gathered their things and left in a taxi for the trip to Lothe. It would take thirty minutes to get there. The sun, now peeking through the clouds, warmed the chill in the air. It was a quiet ride. Sophie looked out the window as they passed through small residential towns. Houses were packed together like books on shelves, washed in colors of peach, purple, and yellow. Max pondered over their chance of winning while twiddling his thumbs. Dr. Becker looked through his notes for the court. They were all too nervous to talk.

None of them noticed the car following behind them. It was none other than that the pushy newspaper reporter. He had seen Max earlier as he wandered through the hotel lobby. He saw them getting into the taxi, and he jumped into his car in pursuit, determined to get his interview.

Max grew impatient. The taxi driver kept circling the streets of Lothe, then finally pulled alongside the curb to call in for directions to the finance court. They had already passed the large old brown-brick building. It was tucked away in a courtyard off a side street.

Dr. Becker tapped the driver on the shoulder, saying, "Drop us across the street. We will walk the short distance to the courthouse."

"Yes, sorry for the confusion."

They gathered their things and piled out of the taxi. When Max stepped into the street to cross it, he bumped right into the nosy young reporter from the café.

"What are you doing here?" Max said. "You are following us. I don't like it." Max could feel his blood pressure rising. They moved back to the sidewalk to avoid getting hit by a car.

"I must get a few words from you, Mr. Diesel, about the case." He shoved a small microphone in his face.

Dr. Becker stepped in front of Max. "Look, we can't say anything about the case now. When we can, you will be the first to know. Give me your card." He stuffed it in his pocket. He signaled to Max and Sophie to cross the street with him.

They left the confused reporter standing there, empty-handed. Frustrated, he sauntered back to his car, planning his next move.

Max was annoyed. Sophie was relieved.

"What a character. So persistent," she said, laughing.

"What a pain!" Max said jokingly.

They walked into the courtyard, putting aside the whole incident. They followed the circular driveway like they were following the yellow brick road with anticipation and caution, stopping in front of the huge old brick building. Engraved in faded gold at the top were the words in large letters: Finance Court.

Max felt beads of sweat at the back of his neck. Sophie felt her heart racing. Max climbed the wide stone stairs to the massive wood door. Sophie was right behind him. When he stopped suddenly, she bumped into him.

"Sorry, Max. I didn't expect you to stop and admire the door."

"It's my fault." He had to run his fingers over the wood door, caressing the detailed carving. "Beautiful work." It was a heavy old wood door with bronze handles. It took his strength and both hands to pull the door open; he held it open for Sophie to enter.

The interior of the building was plain, with high ceilings and stairs to a second floor. It was not as impressive as the outside of the building. A small glass case next to the stairs contained historic books and documents. Black-and-white photographs hung on the walls as well as plaques of state and city coat of arms.

Dr. Becker followed them in, feeling at ease and pleased that they were the first ones there. He pointed to the courtrooms upstairs.

"Elevator or stairs?" Sophie said.

"The stairs, of course," Max said, placing his hand in hers. They paused for a moment, looked at each other, and took a deep breath before slowly climbing the flight of stairs to the top. The youthful Dr. Becker sprinted up the stairs behind them with his long legs and lean body, ready to seize the day.

A notice by the courtroom door displayed the case for the day. Sophie kept staring at it, squinting at first then pouting. She couldn't understand a word. She was becoming totally upset for not learning German.

"Max, read it to me, please, in English."

"Sure, Sophie." He noticed her frustration. "It states that on December 5, 2013, at 9:15 a.m. in courtroom 1, Maximilian Diesel, represented by Attorney Dr. Karl Becker, against the Finance Department of Erfurt.

Residing judges present: Judge Bitter, finance court president; Judge Mintz, finance court judge; Judge Hartz, finance court judge; Judge Lutts and Judge Kronin, volunteer judges."

"Max, it's time. Fate is in our hands."

Chapter 55

Dr. Becker held the door open for Sophie and Max. Startled by the starkness of the room, they stopped before the threshold, their feet glued to the floor.

"Come in. You're not on trial." He grinned at them to calm them down.

"Just a little nervous," Max said, remembering that the last time he had to go to court was to fight for his cabinet.

A reluctant Sophie stepped into the small but organized room. The courtrooms at home, she thought, seemed more intimidating in size and stature—that is, the two she had been in. The morning light from the arched window danced across the room. It warmed her face and body, instantly relaxing the tension she was feeling. Curiosity now replaced the overwhelming feelings of fear and doubt. She was eager to see justice and truth unfold.

Everything was in its place. A gold plaque of the state's coat of arms hung on the back wall behind the judges' black high-back armchairs. The long cherrywood table stood in front of the chairs, and two medium tables stood opposite each other, creating a U shape. The table by the window was for the clerk and her computer. Facing the judges were two small tables, standing three feet opposite each other, where the defendant and plaintiff sat with their attorneys. Three rows of folding chairs were lined up against the back wall. They faced the entire courtroom.

The president of the finance court, Judge Bitter, came over to the three of them. Sophie noticed he was distinguished looking, pleasant, and very tall. Max shook his hand, feeling his hand tremble a little. He expressed how happy he was to be here and have the case heard in court. Dr. Becker extended a firm handshake and a cordial smile.

"We will begin soon," the judge said. "We are waiting for the other judges."

Dr. Becker slipped on his black robe. He looked official and ready to challenge the finance department. He joined Max at the table by the window. The head of the finance department for the City of Erfurt, Dr. Krimpton, and his attorney, Dr. Marta Banck, sat at the table across from them.

Sophie poised herself behind Max. "It's really happening," she whispered, leaning over his shoulder.

Max turned to her as he fussed with his jacket and tie. "Sophie, I am nervous. I hope I remember my notes."

"You will, Max. You always come through when it matters. It's almost over." She flashed a big smile and wished him good luck.

"Thanks." He felt a tightening in his throat.

Six other people sat several chairs away from Sophie. There was the former director of the Gera Museum, Dr. Morgan, a city attorney, an attorney from Erfurt's cultural department, two attorneys representing the Dresden Museum, and finally an art historian from the Dresden Museum.

Max whispered in Karl's ear, "I wonder why Morgan is here."

"I'm not sure. Let's see if he has something to say."

After formal introductions were made, they all sat down to wait for the judges. Three finance judges in long black robes and the two volunteer lay judges, who did not wear robes, entered the courtroom and settled into their comfortable chairs. Judge Bitter, the head judge, led the proceedings. He studied the room with his eyes, carefully and slowly imprinting each person in his mind.

There was a nervous calm all around the room. The sound of papers rustling, whispers exchanging, and pencils tapping in the background set the stage. Sophie looked at her watch—9:25 a.m. It seemed like an eternity had gone by, not minutes. She noticed the judges, four men and one woman. She wondered how the pendulum would swing.

The head judge stood up and instructed everyone regarding the proceedings. A written summary of the case will be read out loud. The other judges will follow along with this summary in front of them. Dr. Becker, attorney for the plaintiff, Maximilian Diesel, will speak first. Dr. Banck, the attorney for the defense, Dr. Krimpton, head of the finance department of the City of Erfurt, second. Litigation would ensue.

Remaining seated, the second judge read the summary. "This case is about resolving Maximilian Diesel's decade-long struggle with the Gera Museum for either possession of artworks belonging to him or financial compensation. The case involves the seizing and exporting of the private collection of Emil Diesel, Maximilian Diesel's father, by the GDR."

He continued reading. "When the authorities discovered Emil Diesel had acquired a massive art collection totaling over two million East German marks, they accused him of being a commercial art dealer rather than a private collector. Emil Diesel was forced to hand over one million deutsche marks' worth of artwork to pay off his tax evasion debt. According to the GDR, upon Emil Diesel's death in 1975, he still owed 500,000.00 deutsche marks. Selected pieces of artworks were transported to the Gera Museum and Dresden Museum to pay off the rest of his debt despite the heir's willingness to pay off his father's debt so that he can rightfully inherit his father's artwork. There was no recourse under East German law for him to fight what he felt was an illegal taxation and seizure of the artwork."

Dr. Becker addressed the court, stating, "He is fighting it now in a German court of law. Maximilian Diesel wants restitution of the artwork, not the money, and has been willing to settle with the museums from the beginning. The museums have been uncooperative so far. It is very clear in this case I have presented to the court that Mr. Diesel, rightful heir, is entitled to his inheritance—his father's art."

Sophie looked up to the heavens. In a quiet whisper, she said, "Are you listening, Emil?"

Judge Bitter spoke. "This is a very complex case. It is about taxation and antiquities." He brought his attention to Dr. Krimpton. "Explain to me how Emil Diesel was forced to pay a 600 percent tax on his income as a collector and as a dealer at the same time. This is unheard of even in the most incredible tax cases."

Dr. Krimpton balked over his words. "I was not in East Germany in 1975. After looking over the case, it seemed like everything was done right. I mean, it was obvious mistakes were made in accounting."

"Mistakes? You call a 600 percent tax bill a mistake?" the judge asked. "I believe it was not a mistake. It appears to me to be intentional."

Dr. Krimpton's mouth dropped, arguing again. "Mistakes were made."

"How can a person be charged twice? Either Mr. Diesel was a collector or a dealer."

All the other judges concurred with Judge Bitter.

Judge Kronin, the volunteer woman judge, agitated by the remarks of Dr. Krimpton, spoke next. "Dr. Krimpton, I am from the former East Germany. Accountants were just as competent as they were in the West. Such mistakes were not made. I concur with Judge Bitter."

Dr. Krimpton stopped talking. He wasn't prepared for this argument. He didn't expect this argument at all.

Sophie could not understand the words, but she observed the manner in which the judge was addressing the defense—the way his voice grew louder and his gestures more precise. It was obvious to her the judge was expressing condemnation. Emil Diesel was wronged, and the taxation was a fraud. She felt goosebumps up and down her arms.

"He believes us. He is going to rule in our favor," she whispered to herself. She wanted to tell Max, but she couldn't. She knew she had to be still.

Judge Bitter addressed the court, looking directly at Dr. Krimpton. "It is my understanding that the plaintiff, Mr. Diesel, wanted to settle with the museums and have his art returned to him instead of receiving financial compensation. I suggest the museums work out a deal with Mr. Diesel. If a settlement cannot be reached, the case will come back to me. I will most likely rule a judgement in favor of Mr. Diesel. The museums will have to give up all the artwork, and financial compensation may be granted as well. It would be foolish not to settle."

Max turned around and caught Sophie's attention. His hands shook, trying to hold back his tears. He was so emotional. Sophie felt her tears running down her cheeks. She knew she was right. She felt it. *They won!*

Max couldn't believe it. Finally, it was over. Dr. Becker was all smiles. He patted him on the back. "It's almost over."

The judge called a recess for fifteen minutes. There was silence as the judges left the room. The attorneys stepped outside to deliberate with one another. Max and Sophie sat alone in the room. They kissed and hugged, still in disbelief. So many years had passed.

Before leaving the room, Dr. Krimpton rushed over to the former director of the Gera Museum, Dr. Morgan, whispering, "You had better tell the Gera Museum and the culture department to settle with them. Otherwise, you will lose everything. The City of Erfurt will not be happy."

Pleased with the outcome, he nodded in agreement. Dr. Krimpton followed Dr. Morgan to make sure he went straight to Dr. Becker for a brief meeting.

Judge Bitter saw Max and Sophie sitting alone in the room. "Mr. Diesel, why aren't you outside with the others?"

Smiling at the judge with ease and relief in his voice, he said, "My attorney can handle everything."

The judge smiled back. He understood.

The session resumed. Judge Bitter addressed the court from his chair. "Have all the parties agreed to the decision to settle?"

"Yes, Your Honor."

"Let us say, by the end of April 2014, if all parties cannot agree on a settlement, the case will come back to me. I will make a final ruling then. I will have a protocol written up for each party involved."

"Thank you, Your Honor."

The judges left. Court was adjourned.

Sophie glanced at her watch. She thought, *It was only two hours. It seemed like forever.*

Dr. Becker turned to Max. "Let's get some lunch."

All nodded in agreement. They walked to a small quaint nearby tavern. The ten-minute walk gave each of them time to reflect and to decompress.

Seated at their table, relieved that court was over, they raised their wine glasses.

"To Emil. He would be proud!"

Max and Sophie raised their glasses to Karl. "We could not have won our case without you. Thank you for your passion and perseverance."

Karl smiled back at his new friends. "Thank you for your patience. Don't worry about the press. It's their turn to wait."

After a good, hearty German lunch, Karl called their taxi to come and get them. Karl and Max were too excited to go back to the hotel. They asked the driver to drop them off at the Gera Museum. Karl wanted to show Max some of his father's inventory they had on display. Sophie was exhausted. She needed to go back to her room and rest. They would meet later for dinner at the restaurant at 1900 hours (7:00 p.m.). They waved goodbye to Sophie and sprinted through the museum doors.

They searched for Emil's pieces and found the exhibit of eighteenth-century German porcelain figurines and the seventeenth-century silver cup on display in cases. They looked until they could look no more. Fatigue set in. They were done for now. As they crossed the old trolley tracks, they discussed the months ahead.

In the hotel lobby, Karl made reservations for 2000 hours (8:00 p.m.). The dining room was full at 1900 hours (7:00 p.m.). Dr. Becker would leave early in the morning and catch the train to Berlin. Max and Sophie would catch the train to Frankfurt in the morning as well.

Max found Sophie asleep. He leaned and kissed her lightly on the forehead. She tossed lightly but did not wake. Max stared at her and thought she was beautiful. She had supported him in every way during their ten-year odyssey. If it hadn't been for her, he would never have pushed to reopen the case. He was so proud of her determination. She believed in him. His memories had held him back at first. In the end, they moved him forward.

He removed his clothes, left them on the chair by the bed, and squeezed in beside her. He felt her breathing, his arm resting over her body. He closed his eyes and fell into a deep sleep.

Hours later, Sophie rocked Max back and forth and said excitedly, "Max, wake up. It is six. Dinner is in an hour."

"No, Sophie. Reservations were changed to eight."

"Thank goodness. We have plenty of time to dress."

"Come back to bed, Sophie."

"We can do it later, Max." She teased him with a flirtatious kiss.

"It's time to celebrate."

She dressed in her shimmering long-sleeved black silk dress, strands of pearls draped around her neck, and wore luscious red lipstick. All eyes were on her.

Max was by her side, this time whispering in her ear, "You look stunning."

She flashed him a big smile. "Thanks."

Karl rose from the table and greeted both of them. He kissed Sophie on each cheek and gave Max a hearty handshake and hug. The champagne was on ice, waiting for them. They toasted to winning their case. They all believed that the judge was amazing. Emil must have been smiling down upon them.

"To Emil!" They raised their glasses to acknowledge his life.

Max remembered the reaction of Dr. Krimpton at the hearing. "He really thought he was going to win. The museums, the city—they all did. The truth prevailed."

A proud smile appeared on Max's face as he confessed to Sophie and Karl, "I have learned so much about my father and myself during these past ten years. I have learned about forgiveness and love, truth and art. Most of all, I understand the undeniable passion behind them all."

They all agreed exclaiming,

"The best is yet to come!"

Acknowledgments

I still cannot believe I had the courage to sit down and write my first novel. Without the support of my husband this novel would not have been written. I am grateful to him for encouraging me to write this story.

I especially want to thank Dr. Ulf Bischof, my cherished friend, for his support and guidance throughout my writing.

I want to thank my teacher Anthony Gangi for inspiring me to keep writing and revising my story until it felt right for me.

I must thank Sally Alexandra Tranos, professional "book doctor," for helping me edit my novel. Her patience and guidance throughout my writing helped me to make it a better story.

Also, to my entire team at Xlibris, who believed in me and helped me publish my first novel, I thank you so much for your continuing support.

Made in the USA
Middletown, DE
21 April 2018